SHADES OF THE HEART

Encounters of the Heart Series - Book 1

Ann Marie Bryan

Victorious By Design
Tallahassee, FL

To order copies of this book, please contact:
Victorious By Design, LLC
P.O. Box 6141
Tallahassee, FL 32314
Lighting the path to your next level

Visit our website at: www.victoriousbydesign.com
Email us at: orders@victoriousbydesign.com

Cover photo courtesy of bigstockphoto.com
Cover creation by Global Multi Media Enterprises (GMME)

ISBN-13: 978-0985146856
ISBN-10: 0985146850

DEDICATION

I dedicate this book to my wonderful mom, Mrs. Estrina Johnson and my six gorgeous sisters.

- Mrs. Icylin Morgan (Sister Mary, my second mom)
- Ms. Beverlyn Johnson (Sister Della)
- Dr. Henritta Stewart (Sister Henny)
- Mrs. Ivalyn Moses (Lee)
- Mrs. Navlet Miller
- Mrs. Verna Thomas

You are all amazing women. I am so blessed to have all of you in my life.

CONTENTS

ACKNOWLEDGEMENTS

Many persons contributed to the completion of this book. Thank you so much. Your storehouses will never be empty.

My Heavenly Father, who loves me. Thank you for making my life a ministry for you.

Extra special thanks to the love of my life, Orville. Thanks for loving me and for never ceasing to let me know. I love you!

I am praying for continued blessings on my mom and amazing siblings, whose unending support I can always count on. Thanks for being there through 'thick and thin.'

Mr. George Morgan - You have been a blessing to me throughout the course of my life. Thanks for being my other 'father.'

To my special sisters in the Lord - you know who you are. Thanks for the sisterhood, the testimonies, and words of encouragement.

Thank you to my pastor, Bishop John E. Baker and his anointed wife, First Lady, Elder Ann-Marie Baker, for continuing to impart God's word in my life. Thanks also to my church family, New Hope International Outreach Ministries.

Ms. Sherry Johnson of Tamar Foundation - Thanks so much for providing insights on sexual abuse. I wept during your session but you've certainly raised my level of awareness regarding sexual abuse. May God continue to bless you on your journey.

To two individuals, whose names I will withhold - Thank you so much for sharing candidly with me about being sexually abused. My heart broke as you shared. I am so thankful to God that you are in a better place today.

Melinda Michelle, President and Founder of Global Multi Media Enterprises (GMME) - Thank you so much for your help with designing the interior and cover of this book. God made you special.

Thanks to the member of Tallahassee Authors Network (TAN) Christian Sub-group. Your support means everything to me. You are the best!

I am fortunate to have a great editorial team - Millicent Battick, Melissa Mallory, Ayana Matthews, Candace McCrary, Yamecike McMillan, Icylin Morgan, Paula Owen, Henritta Stewart, and Julianne Veira who helped me to express my ideas. Thank you for your critique, encouragement, and prayers.

ABOUT LOVE

"Love suffers long and is kind; love does not envy; love does not parade itself, is not puffed up; does not behave rudely, does not seek its own, is not provoked, thinks no evil; does not rejoice in iniquity, but rejoices in the truth;" (1 Corinthians 13:4-6)

PROLOGUE

UP IN SMOKE

Blake glanced at his watch and noticed it was 11:06 AM. He decided there and then, he was taking an early lunch. 'Come now or swing by during lunch,' she had said. The gentle sound of her voice had created a heated stir in his body causing his heart to pick up speed. Grabbing his work bag from the floor, he moved quickly through his office door, closed it behind him, and informed his executive assistant he would be out for a while.

He quenched the urge to bolt for the main door to the office. *What would my staff think?* Instead, he walked swiftly across the carpeted floor, attempting to contain the butterflies that monopolized his stomach. His deep baritone voice rang out as he responded to greetings from members of his staff.

Outside the main door to the office, he walked across the tiled floor of the brightly lit foyer to the row of elevators on the twenty-fifth floor at Petrosa International Bank's headquarters. A few minutes later, he exited through the revolving doors of the building and sprinted across the parking lot to his black BMW.

Blake Montgomery was a man on a mission.

Smiling, he pulled out of the parking lot, seemingly oblivious of the magnificent skyscrapers, the huge electronic billboards, and the many tourist attractions in the bustling commercial hub of Orlando, Florida, where he spent most of his work days.

He had been waiting for her call, almost anxiously awaiting the news. He just knew she was planning to break the news in an extraordinary way. After all, Gabrielle was a master at planning mystery dates and she'd tricked him into coming home for "lunch" several times.

She was like that.

His smile widened as he reminisced about their fulfilling lunch dates. 'I am keeping love alive,' she had teased after one of their lunch hour rendezvous.

Half an hour later, he brought his car to a screeching halt in front of a sprawling estate home with a three-car garage and beautiful tropical landscaping. His tie caught in the car door as he slammed it shut. "Not today," he muttered, hastily releasing himself. He ran towards the front door and swung it open. "Honey, I'm home," he yelled, dropping his work bag behind the closed door.

"In the living room, dear," Gabrielle responded.

Blake was 'beside himself' with excitement. He had run at least one stoplight to get home. Smiling, he made a dash for the living room and came face to face with Gabrielle perched on the edge of the couch. Throwing his car keys on the coffee table, he plopped down beside her, grabbed her shoulders, and turned her to face him. "Okay, break it to me gently."

Gabrielle fidgeted with the wedding band on her finger, mixed feelings about the news, still swirling in her head. Finally, she looked in Blake's smiling face, dread twisting her features. "I…Larry, we," then she finally got it out, "I slept with Larry."

Time stood still as her words reverberated in his head with each passing second. "Wha-what?" Blake stammered with unbelieving eyes. He must not have heard her right. But, her distraught countenance assured him that he did.

"I am soooo sorry," she muttered, gazing at the floor.

Loud voices whirled in Blake's head, his heart hammering loudly against the wall of his chest and he opened his mouth but no words came out. Dazed, the dead weight of his limbs caused him to fall backward on the

9

cushions on the sofa. As if that wasn't enough, she turned the dagger, crushing his already wounded heart.

"I have, I have a sexually transmitted disease…Chlamydia," she filled in, still avoiding his eyes. "You need to check yourself."

His ears were filled with the loud gushing sound of his pounding heart. *The Clam!* He shot up from the sofa, sat down again, grabbed her by the shoulders and began mercilessly shaking her. *This must be some kind of sick joke.*

"STOP!" Gabrielle cried out, feeling as if she was about to be snapped in half.

He released her suddenly and let out a gut wrenching cry, collapsing on the sofa. Then, in a fit of rage, he shot up from the sofa, almost knocking over the coffee table as he stormed out of the living room.

Gabrielle reached out a hand to touch him, but stopped short when he wheeled and glared at her, hurling, "Get AWAY from me!" before moving on.

She ran after him. "I need help, Blake," she whispered, her voice diffused with tears. "You know I love you."

"Leave me alone, Gabby," he spat out, reaching for a drinking glass in the kitchen cupboard. *You need help alright.* But, it didn't matter to him. She had hurt him to the core of his being. The anger he felt threatened to explode. *Say you hate me. At least, that would make me feel better.*

"I'm sorry."

Blake glared at her, trying to stop his mind from racing with violent thoughts he didn't know he possessed. "No. Don't apologize," he growled, holding up his hand. "You knew what you were doing." He could barely stand to look at her. He clamped his jaws tight to bite back a bitter retort as he filled the glass with water from the refrigerator. *What else was she hiding?*

He knew she was going to see her gynecologist that morning and he wanted to accompany her, to hear the good news that "they" were pregnant. She had finally agreed that this was the year for them to start a family, and he was hoping today he'd hear the good news that God had blessed their union with a child. He wanted a son, but nevertheless, he'd take a daughter. So much for the good news! Instead, he'd have to get a checkup.

A checkup! He wanted to check out.

He poured the water down his throat then slammed the glass on the cupboard and stormed out of the kitchen.

"Blake!" Gabrielle's heart-wrenching cry stopped him in his track at the entry way leading to front door.

He grunted and spun around to face her. "WHAT?"

She lowered her gaze. She'd never seen him look at her like that...with contempt and disgust. "Please say something," she begged.

His jaw hardened. "Like what, Gabby? Like, it's okay to sleep with Larry Kanate!" He watched her for a moment. "What were you trying to do? Sleep your way to the top?"

His words pierced her heart, sending feelings of deep regret racing through her. "I'm sorry," she said clutching her hands like a wounded animal.

He gave her a cold, contemptuous glare. He had never felt so unprepared in his entire thirty-eight years on earth. Nothing, absolutely nothing prepared him for her revelation. He veered back to the living room to get his car keys.

"He took advantage of me," she whimpered behind him.

Blake dropped on the small sofa and eyeballed her. "Did he rape you, Gabby?"

"He...He..."

"Exactly. I didn't think so."

"It wasn't like that," she pleaded, kneeling before him and wiping her blood-shot eyes. "It only happened once…the day after you left for Atlanta. I had a moment of weakness and Larry took advantage of…" She paused seemingly at a loss for words.

"Moment of weakness?" Blake snapped. He stood and threw his hands in the air, looking down at her. "How many other moments of weakness have you had with other men?"

Gabrielle flinched, her head bowed towards her chest and tears dripped off her chin. "Don't say that. You know I'm not like that. I am sooo sorry. I was feeling so-"

"Geeze, Gabby," Blake hissed, "Why did you have to sleep with another man? We have a great sex life!" His eyes stung with pent-up fury.

Watery eyes met his. "We do, Blake. I didn't sleep with him. He-He forced…me."

Blake barely moved a muscle. "It's now spring, Gabby! Spring! This happened six weeks ago. Were you even going to mention it, if you didn't get Chlamydia?" He folded his hands across his chest and stared at her. "Let me make sure I get this. You said that Larry forced you, yet you didn't mention it to me. Not once! What is going on with you, Gabby?"

A strangled sob escaped Gabrielle and her slender frame hunched in shame. *Help me, Lord! How can I even begin to explain that the weight of my past has finally caught up with me?* "I-I…"

"Gabby, don't." He had heard enough, enough of her pitiful explanation. "This is not what I signed up for," he said, snatching his car keys from the coffee table. He all but bolted for the front door as the crackling sounds coming from his shattered heart whipped into a frightening, spiraling frenzy.

Gabrielle sprung from the floor. "Please don't go," she cried out, her features twisted in anguish.

But Blake didn't look back. He just needed to get out of there. He wanted to be anywhere but in her presence. Thoughts of the many times she'd smiled at him and uttered the words, 'I love you,' ricocheted through his mind. Tears threatened as he recalled telling her that he reserved the word *adore* to describe his feelings toward God, but he was only going to use it this once with her. "I adore you," he told her, smiling as he looked deeply into her beautiful light brown eyes after watching the magnificent sunset on a beach in Jamaica on their first anniversary.

"Blake, please don't leave," Gabrielle called out, trying to stop him before he opened the front door. In desperation, she threw herself on his back, her hands clasping his waist. "Please, please don't leave me." She pressed her head to the back of his neck, her tears dripping on his shirt.

His heart softened, but in the next minute his mind unleashed images of her and Larry Kanate, making out all over her office – the desk, the sofa, and the floor. He stiffened, his hand gripping the door handle. "Let go of me."

"Blake, please," she begged, "please don't leave me."

But all he heard was the chanting in his head; it was getting louder and louder by the second. Thousands of voices chanting - "Betrayal! Betrayal! Betrayal!" Without saying a word, he turned around and put her away from him.

A cool blast of air surged in as he swung the house door open. With tears streaming down his face, he slammed the door behind him and with the click of the lock, he shut Gabrielle out of his life.

"Nooooo!" Gabrielle cried out, crumbling to the floor. The pain in her heart hit an unbearable level and grief consumed her soul as the clicking of the lock reverberated in her ears.

CHAPTER 1

TAKING IT BACK

Seven months later

A muffled groan emanated from Gabrielle's puckered lips as she dropped the basket of dirty laundry on top of the washing machine. *Not in the mood to do laundry. And this rain is not making it any easier,* she mused, glancing out the window. *Did not expect all this rain to kick off the fall season.* A flash of lightning illuminated the laundry room followed by the rumbling of thunder, and she quickly closed the curtains.

She sighed deeply, contemplating her next move when a glimmer of light reflected on her diamond wedding band as her hand rested on the laundry basket. She held up her hand and thoughtfully gazed at her wedding ring. *Will I ever get past losing Blake?* Her heart burned with trepidation and she gulped a deep breath to keep full-fledged panic at bay.

Feeling nostalgic, she headed to her bedroom. Since her separation from Blake, her mind felt like a battlefield. She was constantly putting out one fiery mental attack after another. Granted, she'd faced her fair share of hard knocks in life and had cultivated a protective shell, but this one was different; she had a hand in her downfall…a major hand at that.

Her countenance seemed to condemn her as she walked past the dresser and caught sight of her reflection in the mirror. Her light brown eyes stared back at her, empty and sad. *Will my heart ever recover?* The unhappiness seemed to be eating at her heart, and no doubt would begin to peel away her core if she did not get a firm grip on her life.

Flopping backwards on the gold ruffled bedcover, she encouraged herself, "Stay strong, girl. The Lord is perfecting that which concerns you."

She had laid in bed way too late that Saturday morning, whispering fervent prayers, asking God again to save their marriage. She prayed that her infidelity had not permanently destroyed their union. She remained hopeful since Blake had not filed for a divorce, even though he had moved out.

A sharp pain slowly screeched through her heart as she remembered how Blake desperately wanted to start a family. "Let's start discussing names," he said. His dark brown eyes twinkled as he spoke during their devotion one night as they lay facing each other in bed.

She looked at him, taking in the flawlessness of his chiseled features. Handsome would not aptly describe him. With his caramel complexion, well-toned muscular body suggesting years of working out, and his signature, gap-toothed smile which seemed to say, "The world is a better place because you are in it," he was one tall, good-looking man.

"Gabby?" Blake called out when he noticed that she was staring. "Do I have something on my face?"

"No!" She smiled tenderly at him, caressing his cheek with her hand. "I love you."

He returned her smile, pulling her into his arms and dotting her face with kisses before covering her lips with his own. He kissed her leisurely, then urgently until she arched tightly against him, moaning loudly. Her toes curled and she feverishly clutched his shoulders, quivering and wanting more, demanding more. And he gave her more but not before ripping his lips from hers to say, "I love you."

He understood her well enough to know how to give her the greatest pleasure. She would venture to say, he'd mastered it and thankfully, it was his pleasure too. His rapidly rising desire was as powerful and insatiable as hers. Every moment with him hurled her into a blissful, heated dimension, leaving her feeling completely spent yet breathlessly fulfilled.

She had no doubt that Blake loved her...completely. He never failed to let her know. He had displayed only love and deep admiration for her during their marriage, and many times he had calmed her fears with loving kindness. But, she could not get rid of the feelings of inadequacy that assailed her because of horrible childhood memories.

She let out a deep sigh - a sigh of regret and pain, thinking again about the fateful day when their marriage fell apart, simply shattered before her eyes. Everything about that day was still vivid in her mind.

Early that morning, Dr. Pedro Reyen's assistant had called and told her to visit the office as soon as possible. She had known that something was wrong because she'd been experiencing painful urination and lower abdominal pain. Blake wanted to accompany her to see Dr. Reyen, thinking she was pregnant but she had insisted that it was only a routine checkup and would call him with the diagnosis. He had no idea she had visited Dr. Reyen's office the previous day and was about to pick up her test result.

A chill shot through her as the memory of Dr. Reyen's announcement flashed to the forefront of her mind. She had hung her head in shame when he said, 'You, my dear lady, have Chlamydia.' Her heart sank further by the minute as her doctor droned on about the danger of having the disease. However, he quickly reassured her it was curable and that it didn't do any harm to her reproductive system. But, it was Dr. Reyen's next statement that had caused her to burst into tears, 'Your husband needs to check himself.'

That day, she had decided that going to work was not an option, so she headed home blinded by tears while agonizing about how to relay the news to Blake. The only news he was prepared to hear was, "we are pregnant." Surely, this devastating news would destroy their marriage. Her heart sagged under the weight of the situation and she had contemplated if even she could survive this unwelcomed news.

When she arrived home, she prayed, refusing to let despair claim her thoughts, then she placed a call to Blake. She wished she could tell him over the phone but immediately knew that it would be a bad idea. Instead, she'd told him to, "Come now or swing by during lunch," all the time hoping that the truth would not destroy him.

Kneeling at the sofa in the living room, she prayed a second time and stopped only when she heard the front door open. Blake was home and she was ready…to beg for his mercy.

But mercy was not forthcoming from Blake that day. And, honestly, she didn't expect it would be, at least, not immediately. But, now it seemed not ever.

She rolled on her side wondering how on earth she found herself in such a position with Larry Kanate, to the point where he was now added to her wall of shame, after working alongside him for almost seventeen months.

Why didn't I heed the warning signs?
Did I have some kind of school girl crush on him?
Did I lead him on?
Did I secretly want him?

Ten years her senior, she and Larry had hit it off from the day she had started working at Pallecia Worldwide All Suite Hotel, a luxurious golf and spa resort with the head office located on the outskirts of Orlando. He was Vice President of Human Resources and he had initially hired her as the Human Resources Manager. She was in that position a little over a year and when the Human Resources Director resigned, Larry immediately promoted her to that position after convincing her she was a great fit for the position and he would be on hand if she ever needed help.

On the day of the incident, Larry had passed by her office that morning, and she'd told him she was behind with her part of the presentation for the Board meeting which was happening in two days. Larry volunteered to assist her after work. Nothing strange; they had worked late a couple of times to run over presentations, discuss policy changes or to sort out work related issues.

What was strange though, was as Larry stood talking with her that morning, she'd found herself wondering what he was like at home. Their relationship had been pretty much professional. She remembered even staring at him, a little longer than was considered appropriate and perhaps, for the first time, noticed he was a fine looking forty-five year old. His naturally sun-kissed complexion glowed with vitality. He was all male - physically appealing, tall, and lean. His clean shaven face, highlighted by miniature dimples from a drop dead gorgeous smile, reflected his bold personality and freedom of spirit. He always seemed indomitable, comfortable in any environment and it was fascinating to watch him navigate the political arena at work.

Later that evening, Larry sat across from her, working on a part of the presentation on his laptop while she sat at her desk, working on her desktop.

She walked to the white board hanging on the wall in her office. "I'm seeing where we can cut a bit more cost," she told him, looking at the organizational chart for the newly reorganized advertising division. "Let's merge the positions of Deputy Vice President of Advertising and

Manager of Advertising, and call the new position Senior Manager of Advertising."

Larry drummed his fingers on the arm of his chair, then joined her at the white board to inspect the organizational chart. "Love it."

"That should give us another check mark with the Board," she said, while massaging her aching temples with her fingers.

He smiled at her, taking in her tired eyes. "You need to relax, Gabrielle," he said, touching her shoulder. "You should take off your shoes."

"My shoes...why?" She couldn't quite interpret his gaze. *Was that care in his eyes?*

"Get comfy," he said nonchalantly. "We have another hour or so before we leave."

She sighed. "That may be a good idea." She placed a hand on the white board and almost fell over trying to get out of her pumps.

Larry steadied her. "Here, let me help you." Dropping to his knees, he held on to one of her ankles.

"Oh, okay," she muttered, grabbing his shoulders and wiggling one foot and then the next to help him remove her shoes.

He took his time to remove her shoes before standing. "There, that should help, Shorty."

She grinned at him. "Thanks! Feeling better already. Did you call me, Shorty?"

He chuckled as he moved back to his seat. "I sure did."

She smiled at him. "I'm going to forgive you." She stood at five feet six inches, but he towered above her at over six feet.

His mouth curled in a smile as he removed his tie and threw it on his jacket, which was resting on the chair beside him. "Please...," his eyes fastened on her body as she removed her jacket, exposing her silky red inner blouse neatly tucked in her skirt, "forgive me," he continued, his eyes now resting on his laptop screen.

Smiling, she slid in her chair and was quiet for a moment, clicking away on her desktop. A few minutes later, she stretched her hands above her head and announced, "I'm finished with this part."

"Great!" Larry pinned her with his gaze, then his eyes became fixated on her chest. "You have a nice cleavage," he stated matter-of-factly as if he had complimented her about her hair.

Blushing, she lowered her arms. She had hoped that it was only her imagination when she saw him staring at her chest. "We're tired. Let's finish up tomorrow."

Larry knitted his brows. "Come on, Gabrielle. You're married, so am I, but that doesn't mean I can't admire a nice body when I see one."

She nibbled on her lips as she always did when she was pondering. She didn't want him to feel bad for complimenting her. "Thanks," she said quietly.

"We need a break," he said, sliding out of his chair and opening the small refrigerator in the corner of her office. He motioned for her to join him at the small conference table nearby. "All work and no play makes Gabby a dull girl."

Smiling, she took her seat before him and sipped on a can of Mountain Dew he had placed on the table. "Just what I needed. Thanks!"

He flashed her a triumphant smile, deepening his dimples. "You're welcome!"

She fought the urge to hold his lingering gaze, but failed. He looked great. A *fine specimen of a man*. Her eyes roamed him up and down taking in his raw masculinity. *Why am I admiring Larry Kanate?* She shook her head slightly then took another sip of her drink. *I must be tired,* she rationalized.

"Can't wait for Blake to get back, huh?" Larry drawled teasingly.

The warmth in his voice shot enjoyable tingles down her spine and she lowered her gaze, her confused senses threatening to derail her composure. "Yep! He'll be back in two weeks."

Larry eyed her. "Are you okay? You haven't been yourself all day."

She sighed, her eyes brimming with tears. "I'm okay. I just miss, my Aunt Jean. I could talk with her about anything."

"Life happens," he told her. "But, we know that God is good. He's working everything out for your good." He knew that Aunt Jean was laid to rest two month ago and she was like a mother to Gabrielle. Whatever was bothering her, he was sure she would have talked with Aunt Jean about it.

"Yes. God is good," she agreed, mopping her eyes with a napkin from the table.

"Do you want to talk about it?"

"Not really. But thanks for asking."

"I know exactly what you need," Larry said, feeling an overwhelming need to comfort her. He slid out of his chair and stood behind her. "A massage."

Her brows shot up. "A massage?"

"I'm good at this," he countered, kneading her shoulders with both hands.

Out of reflex, she jumped, grabbing his hands.

"Just relax. Think nice thoughts about Blake," he offered and she relaxed. He continued to gently massage her shoulder and moved to her neck. "You have a tight knot at the base of your neck," he mentioned, keeping his voice impersonal.

She let out a long sigh, closing her eyes as his hands travelled the length of her neck, applying deep pressure. His hands moved to her back and she tensed slightly.

"Relax," he said softly and she did.

Gosh! I miss Blake. I hope we can get past this 'bump in the road' quickly. Why wasn't I honest with him before he found out so callously that I wasn't ready to have a child? Then, before he left for Atlanta, we would have made love and all would be well. Hmmm, passionate love!

Larry gazed at Gabrielle's slightly parted lips, and heat seared through his body. Whatever she was thinking about was causing her to breathe a little heavier. Feeling as if he was committing emotional adultery, he closed his eyes, trying to recall a scripture to clear his mind. At that same moment, an inner voice warned him to stop flirting with temptation.

He opened his eyes and then bit his lips to steady himself, when he realized his hands had taken on a mind of their own and was gently massaging her sides.

"Hmmm," she sighed, arching her chest. He watched her respond to his touch, and he liked that. She made him feel…needed. And when his fingers caressed the base of her breasts with exceeding tenderness, deliberately, teasingly, she shivered. Emboldened by her reaction, he cupped her breasts, and then moaned loudly as his hands melted into their softness.

"Larry!" She flew out of the chair, hugging her chest with her hands.

He followed her closely, then stepped back as she leaned against the wall. For a moment he gazed at her, and the only thing he could think about was his thirst for her…all of her. An inner voice begged him to desist, but his flesh craved her, needed her. And, he had no doubt that he would have her.

"You feel so good," he drawled huskily, his eyes glistening with desire.

She placed her hands on his chest as he leaned towards her. "We...shouldn't."

Larry gazed at her for a second before brushing his lips against hers. "We both need this," he said without hesitation, his mouth temptingly close.

On their own volition, her lips parted invitingly and he eagerly captured her mouth with his, trembling at the velvety smoothness of her lips. Her eyes fluttered shut and she shivered, wrapping her arms around his shoulders as his lips travelled the length of her neck, dropping soft kisses along the way. Just when she could take no more, he lifted his head, his lips hovering above hers. "Absolutely love your lips," he gushed.

She could feel the heat of his breath on her face as she surveyed his lush mouth, his lips beckoning seductively to her. "We...shouldn't," she offered weakly, mesmerized by the aura of his charisma.

Struggling to restrain himself, he silenced her objection by kissing her again, passionately, urgently, and with the confidence of a man who knew what he wanted. Clutching his shoulders for strength, she returned his kiss with more fire than he imagined she would, and his body melted against hers. When he was finally able to pull back, they were both breathing heavily.

"I need you," he whispered, barely able to contain himself.

Their bodies inches apart, he looked into her yearning eyes then brought her hand to his mouth and lightly kissed her knuckles, his warm breath stroking her skin. He released her hand and they stood there, drinking in each other.

She swallowed hard, mumbling, "We need to stop."

He wanted to stop. If only he could tear his eyes away from her lips. "Maybe, just this once?" he asked, his chest heaving in breathless anticipation.

The seconds dragged by as Larry waited for her response. When none came, he turned away from her.

She pushed out a gagged breath. Despite all that just occurred between them, she had to let him know that they should not ever go down that path again. "Lar-Larry," she called out, her voice faint. She was still reeling from the surge of warm, delightful sensations in her body.

In a flash, he swept her into his arms, his body crushing hers. "Your body feels amazing," he said, smiling slightly.

Mercy! I need to fix this quickly. "Thanks," she said softly, nibbling on her lips.

He admired the beautiful pout of her mouth then watched fascinatingly as her lips parted, and she began to speak.

"Larry, we can't-"

Before she could catch her next breath, Larry eagerly and hungrily covered her lips with his. As desire welled up in him, he paused, unsure whether he had her permission to proceed.

She arched closer to him, mumbling, "Let's talk...about this," as a wave of heat enveloped their bodies. Then, she froze, her mind screaming, *No. No. Please don't*, as he lifted her skirt. *This is not happening...not again.* But, she felt powerless to stop him. She heard herself whimper, "Let's...not," but he was too far gone. He intended to have her with or without her consent. She vaguely remembered hearing him whisper, "I won't hurt you," but she definitely recalled praying it would be over quickly. And it was. A few minutes later, he buried his head in her neck, muttering, "Thank you. Thank you."

She was grateful that Larry had pulled away when her tears hit his face. She heard him mumble, "Are you alright?" but she didn't utter a word. Instead, she swiftly pulled down her skirt, retrieved her underwear from the floor then grabbed her purse from the desk drawer before bolting through the office door. And, if she had the physical strength, she would have run the three miles, barefooted, all the way home.

Running seemed to be the ideal thing to do in that moment.

Running from Larry.

Running from herself.

And definitely, running from her past.

That night, she knew she had to stop running, stop running from the ghosts of her past, but she didn't know how to, so she picked up more speed fearing that she couldn't deal with the truth about her life. And by morning, she'd convinced herself that the skeletons of her past and current situations needed to remain hidden and all she needed to do was go on living from day to day.

The heavy drumming of the rain on the windowpane brought Gabrielle back to the present. The gloomy weather seemed to reflect her mood - dreary and sorrowful. She shook her head vigorously attempting to get rid of the overwhelming feeling of doom and gloom, but instead, she unleashed the flood of tears she had been suppressing since she woke that morning. She wished her separation from Blake was only a nightmare, at least then she would wake up and return to her normal life.

A normal life. Now that's a stretch...an unreachable goal.

Her normal life would include Blake.

Plagued with doubts, she mopped her tear-dampened cheeks with tissue from a box on the nightstand then sat up, cross-legged on the bed. *I am not punishing myself anymore. This experience is teaching me exactly what is in me. I must focus on my future…with Blake.*

"I miss him so much, Lord," she murmured. Her cheeks warmed from her memories of him.

She vaulted from the bed, and yelled, "Thank you, Lord, for the victory in my situation," as she headed to the laundry area for a second time. "I am an overcomer," she declared. "My best days are still in front of me."

She dropped the laundry basket on the beige colored ceramic tiled floor near the washing machine. "Yes, they are!" she reaffirmed. A small smile played across her face as she dumped the dirty clothes in the washing machine. *At least, my therapist and the members of my prayer circle think so.*

Despite the frustration and uncertainty that sometimes welled up within her, she was determined to press through the consequences of her action and on the not so great days, she had a few scriptures lined up. Today, she recalled Isaiah 49: 15-16, *"Can a mother forget the baby at her breast and have no compassion on the child she has borne? Though she may forget, I will not forget you! See, I have engraved you on the palms of my hands;…"*

CHAPTER 2

BREAKING FREE

Switching off the ignition, Blake stepped out of his car and caught a whiff of the cool breeze that seemed just right to rejuvenate any mood. His lips tilted upward in a slight smile. *Nothing like the refreshing fall breeze carrying the scent of fresh flowers.* He took his laptop from the back seat, closed the car door and focused his attention on the conversation he was having on his cell phone with Bishop Clandon, the man whom he had leaned on through the most grievous period in his life. Bishop Clandon was encouraging him to return to church.

"Yes, it has been a while," Blake told him as he walked towards the house door.

"Glad you agree," Bishop Clandon quipped. "Now, let me see you put actions behind those words."

Blake couldn't help but smile as he opened the house door and closed it behind him. "Bishop, I will definitely give it some thought."

"Great!" Bishop Clandon encouraged. "Just remember there is no magic to it. Ask the Lord to give you the courage and come on out this Sunday."

"I will, Bishop."

The aroma of delicious food floated through the house, reminding Blake he'd not yet eaten. He made his way to the kitchen assuming that was where he would find Quincy, his brother and Janie, his brother's wife.

"Sounds good," Bishop said. "Have a great evening then!"

"Thanks! Have a great evening too," Blake said before ending his telephone conversation.

He scanned the kitchen and noticed that Quincy and Janie were nowhere in sight, but from the appetizers and entrées laid out on top of the cupboard, it was obvious that Janie was preparing another mouth-watering feast. And, he didn't mind at all…in fact he couldn't wait. It was shaping up to be an amazing evening with all of Janie's delectable must-try seafood dishes.

Grabbing a bottle of Gatorade from the refrigerator, Blake made his way to his bedroom. He placed his laptop, Gatorade, and cell phone on the bed, stripped off his work attire and slipped on a pair of navy shorts and a white t-shirt from the chest of drawers.

After pushing the small sofa near to the bedroom window, he reached for the Gatorade then reclined on the sofa to feel the crisp evening air and savored the stillness and tranquility - the freshness and newness - that he had grown accustomed to.

He was grateful that Quincy and Janie had taken him in after his separation from Gabrielle. They had insisted that he stayed as long as he wanted but he had no intention of overstaying his welcome.

Time to press on, he thought.

He lifted the drink to his mouth and drank some, the liquid sliding down his throat and instantly quenching his thirst. Releasing a grateful sigh, he reclined deeper on the sofa and gazed at the blue sheer curtains fluttering in the slight breeze coming in through the window. He shifted just enough to fasten the curtain securely in the corner of the sofa before mentally going over the telephone conversation he just had with Bishop Clandon. He had not been attending church since his break up with Gabrielle.

"Now that's a change," he muttered, staring at the array of flowers in the garden below the window. He could not remember missing any of the worship services at Greater Love Pentecostal Church since he'd started attending some five years ago. It was time to remedy that…painful as it was about to get when he would have to see Gabrielle face to face. He had not seen her in over six months. Truth be told, he'd been avoiding her. What could he possibly have to say to her? He had nothing to say to her...the woman who had ripped out his heart, and left him for dead, three years, ten months and twenty days into their marriage.

That day, weeping, he'd sped away from their home not knowing where he was heading. Later, he had come to a screeching halt on the side of a highway, blinded by scalding tears. He bowed over the steering wheel, convulsing as loud sobs and wails of anguish escaped his tortured heart. He did not know how long he remained in this mode, but he was dazed and almost collapsing when the overwhelming desire to run hit him. He just wanted to run...and run, hoping that would relieve the unending pain in his heart. He had no idea his heart could hurt so much, crippling him, and leaving him devoid of hope.

In the back of his mind, he knew he needed to reach out for help so he placed a call to Quincy, but couldn't get the words out. Having a coherent conversation was more than his mind could handle. His eyes closed on their own accord as he tried to keep the bile down.

"Where are you?" Quincy asked, concern lacing his voice.

"I don't, don't know," Blake muttered, blinking rapidly in an attempt to clear his sore eyes.

Even in his bewildered state, Blake couldn't miss the urgency in Quincy's voice when he said, "Stay where you are. What do you see?"

"I see a..." Blake paused to adjust his eyes to the early afternoon sunlight so he could see what was before him.

"Any buildings? Any billboards?" Quincy coaxed gently, afraid of what he was hearing in his brother's voice. "Anything?"

"There's a store…can't," Blake muttered, wiping his eyes with his hands, "can't make out the name."

"Anything else?"

"In the distance…" A choked sound ripped from Blake's throat as he attempted to answer. His eyes brimmed with tears and he wiped them away with his knuckles. "There's a… tall yellow building with-"

"A red roof and an orange crane at the front."

Blake squinted against the harsh glare of the sunlight, until his vision finally normalized. "Y-yes."

"Stay right where you are. Coming to get you."

"It's okay. Will …"

"Stay, Blake. I'll come to you."

"K." Blake let out a deep guttural sigh as fresh tears cascaded down his cheeks. He quickly disconnected the call and dropped the phone in the cup holder, not wanting Quincy to hear his pitiful sobs. A wave of tiredness washed over him and he placed his head on the steering wheel and allowed the tears to flow.

And, it was in that same position that Quincy found him, when he alighted from a taxi, an hour later. He knocked on the window and motioned for Blake to unlock the door.

Blake did so without saying a word. The only thing on his mind was to crawl into a hole and never ever come out.

Quincy fought back tears that threatened to blind him, when he saw Blake's swollen eyes and broken countenance. He helped Blake out of the car then made sure he was secured in the passenger seat before walking around to slide behind the steering wheel. Although Blake was no longer making any of those terrible sobbing sounds, he was gazing through the windshield like a wounded animal.

Quincy placed a comforting hand on Blake's shoulders as fresh tears rolled down his cheeks. "Let me get you out of here," he stated quietly, wondering what could have happened that had caused Blake to park on such a busy highway, way over an hour from home.

Half an hour later, Quincy pulled into a parking spot at a public park. He had kept a watch on Blake out of the corners of his eyes. All the attempts to garner information from him, proved futile. Blake was only willing to utter, to spew out one word, 'NO,' when Quincy asked, "Should I take you home?" Quincy concluded something was horribly wrong on the home front.

It was Blake who broke the silence as they sat there. "Can't talk about it, Q," he said, releasing a broken sob.

Quincy looked at him trying to decide how best to handle the situation. "Would you like to stay with us tonight?"

Blake nodded without looking at him.

"Okay. You don't have to talk about it if you don't want to," Quincy assured him before pulling away.

A week later, Blake knew that he needed professional help because he was still having trouble sleeping. The tears had stopped somewhat, but the pain in his heart refused to go away. He felt the need to talk, yet he also wanted to be alone, wanting to wallow in self-pity. But, he knew professional help was the right way to go so he placed a call to Bishop Robert Clandon in the wee hour of the morning. And, ever since that day, Bishop Clandon had been his confidant, lifting him up in prayer and offering wise words of counsel.

The following week, Blake returned to work and working became an obsession...mostly to get his mind off his situation. Then, much to the surprise and joy of his staff, he announced he had decided to spearhead the Information Technology project team which was heading the following week to the new branch of Petrosa International Bank in Wichita, Kansas.

As Vice President of Information Technology, he was heavily engaged in this four-month project which kept him busy in the days. Nights were the hardest, tossing and turning when thoughts of Gabrielle's betrayal filled his mind. He waited as long as he could before going to bed, but when he did doze off, he would jump out of his sleep, in cold sweat, and he would spend the rest of the night hoping for daybreak.

After the project ended, he'd taken two months of vacation leave, still trying to sort out his life. Like a zombie, twice a week during lunch time, he attended counselling sessions with Bishop Clandon.

There were days when he didn't know whether he was going or coming, and Bishop Clandon would be a shoulder to cry on.

Blake shook his head as memory after memory assailed him then settled on a particular Wednesday lunch time session he had with Bishop Clandon, when thoughts of Gabrielle's unfaithfulness ravaged his mind. "This must be someone else's life," he had muttered between sobs as he slumped over the side of a chair in Bishop Clandon's office at church. "The joke is going on and everyone gets it but me. Everyone! I feel like I have a big stamp on my forehead saying, 'BETRAYED' and everyone knew about it long before I did."

Bishop Clandon allowed him to talk and when he could get a word in, Bishop spoke, "I know it hurts, but you will get through this. Yes, you will. I declare it in the name of Jesus."

But during that season, he was definitely living inside his head, inside his pain. "This is my house. My castle. I got invaded from the inside," he uttered in disbelief. He stood and began pacing then stopped to face

Bishop Clandon. "I keep visualizing what she and that, that... man did. How they did it. Where they did it. It's driving me crazy." He plopped down on the chair and covered his face with his hands as fresh tears started to flow.

Bishop Clandon walked over to him and placed his hand on his shoulder. "I know you've been through a lot, but don't keep torturing yourself, thinking like that. It's hard now, but you will survive this."

"But, how?" He looked at Bishop Clandon, his watery eyes filled with anxiety. Yet, he did not wait for an answer. "You know what I wonder, did I push her to do this? Did I not spend enough time with her? Did she want something new?"

"It will become clearer, son. Let us ask the Lord for clarity and strength for you as you go through this challenging time." With that, Bishop Clandon held on to his hand and kneeled and prayed until the peace of God swept through his heart.

The beeping of Blake's cell phone pulled him back to the present. He gazed at the phone on his bed. The beep was a reminder to prepare for his early morning teleconference with the Information Technology project team at Petrosa International Bank in Wichita, Kansas. A slight smile curled his lips. He enjoyed working with the Wichita team.

A gust of cool breeze blew the curtain over his head and he placed the Gatorade on the ground and fastened the curtain again in the corner of the sofa before taking his seat. He heaved a deep sigh. "How did my life get so complicated?" he muttered, stretching his arms above his head. *One minute I am awaiting good news and the next minute I'm cancelling anniversary plans for Hawaii and being treated for Chlamydia.*

Gabrielle was the real planner in the family but she'd let him do their anniversary planning, at least for the time being. He felt pretty good about what he'd done so far. They both liked to travel so on their first anniversary they visited Jamaica, on the second Canada, and on the third Grand Cayman. He had made great plans for their anniversary celebration in Hawaii, but their fifth anniversary would have been the kicker - a celebration in Paris, the "City of Love."

How did we end up...just drifting?
Was I that blind?

It had bothered him when he had to leave her so early in the year to make the business trip to Atlanta but when he'd returned, he was happy that she had taken time off from her busy work schedule and was home. He was tired of seeing her stressed out from her new position which she had gotten late last year.

Almost two weeks after he had returned from Atlanta, he celebrated with her when she got a new job which she thought would be less demanding, even though she would be making the same salary.

Life was great all around. She had apologized again for lying about not being on contraceptive, and he forgave her because he'd already purposed in his heart in Atlanta to do so. They restored their prayer sessions at home and their once a week date night was definitely happening.

And, he was happy in the bedroom too. Back then, because of her hectic work life, she almost had him on a schedule, and he hated it. He'd missed being able to make love to her whenever and wherever he wanted to. And, he did just that - slowly, intensely and passionately, anytime the opportunity presented itself. Truth be told, he'd skillfully arranged many such opportunities. And she knew the signal. From that special gaze, instantly, she knew what he wanted, felt what he wanted; it was on full display. In those beautiful moments, their bodies united, only to explode with passion and fire until they were deliriously satisfied.

Unforgettable memories, Blake thought, and then stiffened as he caught himself. *That was then.* And, he certainly had no intention of ever putting himself in a position where his heart would be torn into tiny pieces in a matter of seconds. Once was enough. He couldn't believe he had been such a fool, believing Gabrielle's declarations that she loved him and had his best interest at heart. Sure, he wasn't perfect. Far from it. But, he didn't think she would ever treat him that way.

That's all past, he reminded himself. *No one will EVER get the chance to break my heart again.*

The distant echoes of a thunder roll reminded him he'd already passed the worst. No need 'crying over spilled milk,' he told himself as he took another sip of Gatorade. Suddenly, gratitude washed over him and he mentally thanked God that he was finally picking up the pieces. It took him a while but he had resumed some semblance of normal life, and in a few minutes, he was going to continue apartment hunting and hopefully soon he would take his life to the next level.

He got up and retrieved his laptop from the bed to begin working on documents for his meeting, when he heard knocking on his bedroom door.

"Come in!" he responded.

"No need!" Janie yelled behind the closed door. "Dinner will be ready in ten minutes."

"Thanks, Janie!" he hollered back smiling.

Janie had literally insisted that the household have dinner together when they were home. But Blake figured that Quincy's compassionate wife was simply making sure that he did not return to the solitary, lonesome "soldier" that he'd become when he'd first taken up refuge in their home. A confident grin crept across Blake's face as his laptop powered up. *That was the old Blake.*

CHAPTER 3

FACE TO FACE

"Blake," Gabrielle murmured. "Turn his heart towards me, Lord. I need him." Oh how, she missed him - his joyful laughter and steady perspective on life. She nibbled on her lips for a moment. *I wonder if he ever thinks about me.* Tears stung behind her eyes and she fought to keep them at bay.

"I am courageous," she declared boldly, peering closely at her reflection in the mirror on the dressing table. She adjusted a strand of hair behind her ear, and then pulled on her black and white fitted cap-sleeve, side-draped dress, to set it in place on her body. After glancing at her t-strap, black and white zebra high heel shoes, she took her black purse from the bed and headed to her car.

Today, she had to face Blake at church.

Communication between her and Blake had literally been non-existent. All her efforts to reach out to him were met with coldness…actually, more like an arctic blast. She shivered involuntarily, remembering how distant he sounded on the phone. Yet, she couldn't blame him. What she had done to him was dreadful. He didn't deserve that.

He had returned home the weekend after their argument to move out some of his things and he had gruffly told her he was staying with Quincy and Janie. Two weeks later, while she was at work, he picked up his mail and moved out more of his clothes from the walk-in closet in their bedroom.

Each month, he mailed her a check to help cover the bills and on two occasions, he'd left bags of oranges for her on the kitchen table, which she knew he'd collected from his parents' orchard.

Urgently needing divine guidance, Gabrielle prayed for strength as she drove to church. By now their separation was obvious to her fellow church members. For months, she'd tried her best to ward off any questions concerning Blake during his long absence from church, but she had not deluded herself into thinking that there weren't wagging tongues since Blake had been missing for quite some time. A few church members often looked at her as if she was someone to be pitied. Yet thankfully, there were also sympathizers in the congregation, and she was glad for their mostly indirect approaches. She saw the support in the warmth of their gazes, in the brightness of their smiles, and felt it in the warmth of their embraces and words of encouragement. They were praying and cheering for her.

Last Sunday, she spotted Blake from the parking lot when he had returned to church for the first time since their separation. But seeing him standing outside the main entrance to the sanctuary, talking with a small group was too much for her to handle. Her heart begun to shudder wildly and when she thought of exiting her car, her heart palpitations grew stronger. She just couldn't drive back the instinct to flee. So, she didn't give herself a pep talk, didn't try to call Vivian, didn't consider if anyone saw her; she simply waited until he walked through the entrance door before driving away. Running was a spineless action, but she just had to save herself. She had no desire to play the hypocrite, pretending all was well in her world by offering gracious smiles.

Later that day, she had heard through Vivian that he was royally welcomed back by Bishop Clandon and pretty much all who were participating on the program for the worship service that Sunday.

Gabrielle smiled. *No doubt squeals of delight had gone up from the congregation as one of their favorite 'sons' had returned.* According to Vivian, he'd smiled, bowed deeply, then lifted his hands in praise to the Lord. Vivian also told her that Blake did not play the keyboard or sing with the Praise and Worship team but instead spent the time assisting in the audio booth.

Gabrielle pulled into a parking space at church and surveyed the scene before coming out of her car. *Phew.* Blake was nowhere in sight. She gracefully alighted from her car and walked purposefully across the parking lot into the sanctuary in search of Vivian.

Waving at a few members of the congregation who were huddled in a conversation, she was scanning the sanctuary for Vivian when she caught sight of Blake on the altar placing the microphones in the stands. *Go! Go now!* An inner voice urged, but she stood there transfixed, watching him, her heart thudding away. She held her breath as he turned and looked at her for a few seconds before lifting a hand to say hello. She stiffened then motionlessly lifted a hand in response before turning away.

Dazed and confused, she rushed to the restroom in the foyer then locked herself in one of the cubicles. Leaning against the wall, she attempted to process her racing thoughts. Her cell phone beeped and she reached for it in the side of her purse. A sigh of relief left her. It was Vivian.

"Girl, I need you," Gabrielle disclosed hastily.

"Been looking for you," Vivian said in a hushed voice. "Just spoke with Blake. He is-"

"I can't be here, Viv," Gabrielle blurted out, cutting her off before she could finish speaking.

"It's going to be alright," Vivian told her gently. "Meet me in the first parking lot."

"Okay."

Gabrielle cautiously opened the bathroom door and her eyes flitted through the foyer, to make sure Blake was nowhere in sight. She greeted a few people before exiting to find Vivian, her childhood friend whom she knew she could talk to about anything. Both only children, they operated like sisters, from high school through college and now into adulthood.

Her eyes flitted around the parking lot in search of Vivian and she saw her signaling by waving her hand.

"Gabs, it is well," Vivian encouraged when she stood before her. "You were going to see him sooner or later." Vivian held Gabrielle's hands. "Nooooo. No tears this morning," she said, reaching into her purse and handing Gabrielle a napkin. "It will all work out. You know God is…" Vivian paused abruptly.

Gabrielle stopped dabbing her eyes, and knitted her brows. "What's wrong?"

Vivian eyed her. "Look at me," she tugged at Gabrielle's hand. "I repeat, look at me. Do not look around. Get yourself together."

Gabrielle's eyes widened.

"Blake is heading towards us," Vivian told her.

Gabrielle squirmed and Vivian shot her a warning look. "Shush! Maintain your composure and let me handle it." She released Gabrielle's hand, and with an entreating look told her in a low tone, "Relax you face. He's near. Focus on our conversation."

Gabrielle's heart beat wildly in her chest and she felt breathless. "Okay."

"Great!" Vivian smiled at her. "So, we're looking for a keynote speaker for the women's session at the Family Life Conference. If you can recommend anyone, let me-"

"Hi, ladies," Blake's husky voice interrupted Vivian. He slowed down just enough for them to respond.

"Happy Sunday," Vivian responded pleasantly, while Gabrielle attempted a smile.

Blake smiled slightly at them before moving towards his car at the far end of the parking lot.

"Give me a moment," Vivian told Gabrielle, opening her car door in a bid to stall for time until Blake was out of earshot. She grabbed a book from the back seat and locked the door. "Let's go."

"I want to go home," Gabrielle muttered, staring at Blake's back.

"He's going to turn around and see you staring at him. Come on." Vivian tugged her arm and they move towards the foyer.

"Viv, I need to go home. I can't do this. I need to find another church."

"I know it's hard but you know you can't run away. Stay rooted and let God direct your steps."

Gabrielle's eyes rolled on their own accord, before her brows crumpled in a frown. "He'll be singing with the Praise and Worship team. What do I do? Keep my eyes shut?" She didn't want to be disagreeable but she couldn't stop herself.

"Listen to yourself. Hold it together. You can do this," Vivian said, peering at her. "Anyway, he's not singing. He's helping out in the audio booth so you won't be able to see him, unless you are at the front to the middle of the sanctuary."

"Now that's a relief. I'll sit near the back and don't expect to see me after church. I'll be slipping away."

"Okay," Vivian pursed her lips. "I'll be praying for you. You know that's no way to win back that man."

Gabrielle hung her head. "Yes. Pray for ya Sister."

Vivian hugged her waist and they moved through the foyer to the sanctuary.

CHAPTER 4

UNSOLICITED MEMORIES

"Dinner was superb. Thank you!" Blake smiled at Janie across the table. It was now a given that she expected him to be at the dinner table, especially on Sundays.

"You are welcome." Her cheeks glowed as she grinned at Blake, her dimples deepening. "Just a little something I threw together to brighten your Sunday afternoon." Her charming, vivacious, larger than life personality shone through as she spoke.

"Threw together?" Blake countered with raised eyebrows. "Janie, you are a master chef. This Hawaiian Pineapple Chicken was no joke. It was mouth-watering, finger-licking good."

Janie smiled at him. "You are sooooo good for my ego. Please stick around!"

Blake chuckled. "I sure will, if you keep cooking like this."

Quincy cleared his throat and looked pointedly at Janie. "You never tell me to stick around." His frame was still dressed in the black tailored suit, white shirt, and red tie that he wore to church. His wavy black hair, combed sleek to the back of his head, highlighted his smooth, dark complexion.

Janie landed him a charming smile. "Darling, because you live here! And, let me hasten to say, I would have it no other way."

"You are giving me heart palpitations," Quincy said clutching his chest.

"Then you are alive." Janie grinned at him. "Now, that's a good thing."

After twelve years of marriage, anyone who spent time with Quincy and Janie knew they doted on each other, like every day was their honeymoon. She kept him on his toes and he wouldn't have it any other way. It was no wonder almost five years ago that Janie almost lost her mind when she couldn't hear from Quincy for an entire day after he left home on a four-day business trip. She became hysterical, thinking Quincy had died, but before night fall, she'd received a call from Quincy's boss informing her that Quincy was in a car accident and was in the hospital.

"Do you need seconds, love?" Janie's petite, slightly chubby frame leaned over the table as she spoke to Quincy, who looked lovingly at her from the head of the table.

Quincy nodded vigorously, releasing the charming Montgomery gap-toothed smile. Beyond the differences in their personalities, he and Blake were unmistakably brothers - closely matched in facial features, height and physique.

"That would be a yes," Blake said, chuckling as he watched Quincy.

A pleased smile appeared on Janie's face as she began to lay out seconds on Quincy's plate.

"Yum!" Quincy beamed.

They truly enjoyed each other's company, Blake thought, watching their interaction. "When did you cook, Janie?" Blake asked. "Thought you guys went to church."

"Oh, we went to church alright. I slipped out as soon as church ended. I had to grab Quincy by the hand. You know how Elder Quincy Montgomery loves to greet everyone before he leaves church." Jolly laughter rang out from her. "Happy to report we were not the last ones to leave church today. Thanks to me!"

"Come on, babes!" Quincy touched her hand. "Admit it. You like to greet the church folks too."

"I sure do!" Janie responded. "But today, I was on a mission."

"Glad you were," Blake chimed in. "I was spiritually fed and now I am physically fed. Couldn't ask for more."

"Happy I could help." Janie smiled at him, and then looked towards her husband. "Now for some R and R."

"Yes!" Quincy agreed.

"I'll do the dishes," Blake volunteered.

"Oh! You don't have to," Janie said.

Blake looked at her with mock sternness, before getting up and grabbing a few dishes from the table. "I insist. That was my duty at …" Warmth crept up his cheeks as he caught himself when he realized he was about to say home.

"Go ahead, Bro," Quincy filled in quickly, downplaying what just happened.

That was just like Quincy, always protecting his younger brother. They were ten years apart and when they were younger, their mom and dad had assigned him to be Blake's guardian. He took his job seriously and they had been close ever since.

"My pleasure," Blake responded, escaping to the kitchen with a pile of dishes. He placed the dishes in the sink then briefly squeezed his eyes shut. "Pull it together," he quietly scolded himself before returning to get the rest of the dishes.

By the time Blake returned to the dining room, Janie had left the table and Quincy was gathering up some of the plates. He glanced at Blake, "I know you volunteered to do this. Just helping you get these dishes to the sink."

"Okay. Thanks!"

When they had finished clearing the table, Quincy leaned against the refrigerator observing Blake as he washed the dishes.

"You don't have to be strong all the time," Quincy said quietly. "It's okay to miss her." He wanted to say more but he knew Blake was not in the frame of mind to hear what he had to say. Although he did not know all the details about what had occurred between him and Gabrielle, he had wept and prayed alongside Blake after he had driven him home from the busy highway on that fateful day. He wished Blake would share more with him, especially regarding how he was coping on his own. But each time he attempted to bring up the subject, Blake was tight lipped, no doubt still hurting. And, understandably so.

Blake forced his body not to tense, something that usually occurred at the mention of anything to do with Gabrielle. "If you say so," he murmured, not looking at Quincy.

"Why won't you talk with me about it, Blake? I am not the enemy."

"There is nothing to talk about." Blake looked at him. "I know you're not the enemy, Q. I can't thank you and Janie enough for accommodating me here."

"You are welcome. Stay as long as you want."

"Thanks…" Blake paused to gather himself, "for your help during this turbulent period in my life. I appreciate you and Janie for not prying and also for your generosity when I needed it most." He sighed, placing the glass he seemed to have been rinsing forever in the dish tray beside the sink. "Nevertheless, I have to move on. As you know, I have been scouting out apartments."

"It's our pleasure to help," Quincy confirmed, smiling. "We're really glad you are here. You can stay as long as you want to."

"Thanks," Blake said, concentrating on washing the dishes.

The quietness in his voice touched Quincy's heart. He just hated to see Blake trying so hard to be brave when he was hurting so much. To others looking on, he would seem okay but Quincy knew his little brother only too well. In one of their brief conversations, Blake had told him that he had forgiven Gabrielle, but Quincy knew Gabrielle was well embedded in Blake's daily life and without her, he was like a 'fish out of water.'

"Was Gabrielle at church today?" Quincy asked, still pressing for a conversation.

"Yes," Blake answered without any trace of emotion.

"Did you speak with her?"

"Not really…Kind of."

Quincy knew that their conversation was over so he patted Blake on the shoulder and left the kitchen.

Blake let out a sigh of relief. He was not in the mood to talk about his situation with Gabrielle, and he felt bad for not divulging more to Quincy because he knew that Quincy cared. While he knew he'd covered a great distance on the road to recovery, he still felt emotionally frail when it came to any conversation regarding Gabrielle.

His brows furrowed after he turned off the faucet and reached for a sheet of paper towel to dry his hands. *Why was she in such a hurry to leave church?* He was standing at the back of the sanctuary when he saw her quickly making her way through the crowd before exiting through the side door. *Why do I even care?*

He walked into his bedroom, propped himself upon the pillows, and then turned on the TV. After flipping through a few channels, he settled on CNN. As he stared blindly at the TV screen, unconsciously, his mind kept rolling back to Gabrielle and many questions concerning their break-up blazed in his heart.

What if he'd questioned her about her reason for continuing to take contraceptives?

What if he'd not been so focused on his own needs?

What if he'd forgiven her and made love to her before he'd left for Atlanta?

What if he had obeyed the scripture? - "Be angry, and do not sin: do not let the sun go down on your wrath."

Their argument seemed so stupid now. He remembered how he couldn't wait to get home from work that day. He was looking forward to making love to her, at least once that evening, and spending quality time with her before he left for Atlanta in the morning. Whenever he was going on his business trips, she would gladly come home early from work to prepare for him.

That day, Gabrielle was ready for him, all laid out on their king-size bed in his favorite baby pink satin negligee, smiling at him. Her eyes were filled with fire that he had grown accustomed to. His body hardened with fierce longing as he watched her and he rushed to the bathroom to take a quick shower before melding his body to hers.

"Been thinking about you all day," she told him, kissing him softly and making him groan in pleasure.

His hands lovingly caressed her cheeks then travelled down her chest and she shuddered, her body reeling with desire.

"I want you," he murmured passionately, nibbling her neck then arresting her mouth with his. He loved her mouth - full and irresistible lips that mesmerized his senses with their touch. His whole body trembled appreciatively as she wrapped her arms tightly around his neck, and continued to kiss him with growing passion and without inhibition, her body pliable and urgently needy against his.

Suddenly, he felt her tugging at his shoulder, almost desperately.

"I need a moment," she puffed out, when he finally pulled his mouth away. "Don't move. I'll be back in a minute."

He gazed at her then masterfully kissed her a second time, before rolling off her.

She slid off the bed and raced to the bathroom and he heard the sound of the closet door opening, then silence.

What in the world is she doing? Curiosity got the better of him and he walked in the bathroom and apparently startled her, because she gasped and a small packet fell from her hand as she attempted to close her 'comfort' box. They both reached for the packet and he picked it up - *A packet of oral contraceptives!*

He eyed her in disbelief. "What is this?"

She froze, guilt spreading across her face. "Blake, I-I-I'm-"

"Why would you lie to me, Gabby?" His mouth pressed tightly, he studied her as if seeing her for the first time. "What else are you hiding in your 'comfort' box?"

She had a white rectangular shaped gift box which she told him contained 'girly' stuff from her childhood days. He had never seen the contents, but a few times, he'd caught her looking in the box with a gentle gaze, before securing the box cover in place with a piece of twine. He had taken to calling it her 'comfort' box.

Gabrielle's gaze dropped to the floor. "Blake, I'm not hiding anything. I just-"

"It's okay. No need to explain." He walked out of the bathroom.

She dropped her 'comfort' box on the counter and ran after him. "I'm sorry. I-I-"

"Forgive me for wanting to start a family, Gabby," he said angrily, glaring at her. "For wanting to do what every other couple on the planet is doing."

"Blake, please. This is my last month on contraceptives."

"Okay," he said calmly, sliding under the bed covers. "Let's call it a night. I'm leaving early morning."

She'd stared at him momentarily, before walking back to the bathroom, no doubt in tears. He barely slept that night and knew she didn't either.

Early the next day, he'd rushed from the kitchen into their bedroom to say goodbye, but he could barely contain himself when he found her sitting cross-legged on the bed, a strap of her negligee resting on her arm as she leaned over her devotional guide. In a split second, heat coursed through his body and he drew in a deep breath. Captivated…as always. His eyes travelled to the soft mound of her breasts then moved to her lovely dark brown hair cascading over her shoulders, and complementing her gorgeous honey brown complexion. Incredibly beautiful didn't even come close to describing her. He gazed at her for a moment longer than he intended before finally catching himself at the sound of her voice.

"Good morning, honey," she said, giving him a slight smile.

"Good morning," he responded, moving to pick up his work bag and suitcase from the foot of the bed. "I'm leaving. I'll let you know when I get there," he told her as he turned towards the bedroom door.

"Let's pray before you leave," she said.

He stopped in his track. They always had prayer times, even though it seemed they were slacking off these days. Partly because of his hectic church schedule and her recent promotion, which at times had caused her to work late hours. The prayer, he definitely welcomed, but he didn't know if he had the self-control to resist her. Just one look at her, made every part of his anatomy do the 'happy dance,' and he'd gotten use to capitalizing on the rapid shift in his body temperature that her presence prompted.

I am still mad at her, he rationalized. *That will keep my head straight.*

After placing his work bag and suitcase on the floor, he sat on the edge of the bed and she stretched out both hands to hold his. The other strap of her negligee slid from her shoulder, exposing more of her twin peaks, and he sucked in his breath and squeezed his eyes shut. He attempted to focus his thoughts as she prayed for his safety and their marriage.

"Amen," she said softly, at the end of the prayer.

"Amen," he agreed, opening his eyes to find her staring into his. Before he could move, she cupped his face between her hands and did what she'd always done, kissed one cheek then the next, then pecked softly at his lips before kissing him as if there was no tomorrow. He grabbed handfuls of the bedcover on either side of him, then gave up and drew her tightly against him as his temperature soared.

"I am mad at you," he protested through an inaudible moan, returning her kiss with matching passion and wanting more.

She came up for air and wrapped her arms around his head, burying his head between her breasts.

A tug-of-war took place within him. He really needed to have his fix that was cut short last night.

"I love you," she whispered, aching with longing. When no response came, she released him. "Have a great trip."

He could barely move, didn't want to. Finally, he pulled himself together. "I'll let you know when I get there," he told her, heading to the door.

For so many reasons, he knew he needed to go back to her, but he was still mad. Mad at her for lying to him. This was the year they'd agreed to start a family. After grabbing his work bag and suitcase, he walked out of their bedroom.

Blake felt warm, just thinking about that morning. But he quickly dismissed his thoughts, reprimanding himself for his weakness and the unbridled walk his imagination had taken. He took up the remote which was beside him on the bed and switched off the TV before sliding off the bed and sitting on the small sofa near the window.

Running his hands over his face, he reclined on the sofa, trying to shake off warm thoughts about Gabrielle. But, his mind still rested on her. He missed her in so many ways - her rare intelligence, her effortless kindness, her sense of humor, and her spontaneity. He admired her unique ability to brighten any room she occupied with her infectious smile and positive attitude. Their witty banter, carefree romps, and especially their thought-provoking devotions, always made him long to be in her presence. He could hardly believe their marriage had dissolved to polite, tight-lipped smiles between each other.

He stared at the white clouds through the window, realizing that for the first time since their separation, he caught himself seriously thinking about Gabrielle. He steeled himself against further compassionate and sentimental thoughts. *I dare not trust her...again.*

CHAPTER 5

LETTING IT GO

A feeling of loneliness washed over Gabrielle and she closed the Women's Devotional Guide that she was attempting to read and rolled on her side on the bed. Her thoughts spun in circles about her separation. *I miss him so much - our lively devotions, our stimulating conversations.* A smile touched her lips. *He was pretty pleasing to the eyes too.*

She placed the devotional on the nightstand and turned off the bedside lamp, hoping to fall asleep soon. "My sleepless nights are over," she declared, fluffing the pillow before laying her head on it. *Had way too many of those. And, I refuse to go to work tomorrow looking all worn-out.* She sighed, remembering her nights of tossing and turning all too well.

After Blake left, she'd spent many nights curled up on her bed crying, with her hands tightly wrapped around a long ivory pillow, and her 'comfort' box nearby for company. *I have to find a way to let go,* she thought during that season. But, she was not ready, far from being ready to let go.

Two weeks after her separation from Blake, Vivian visited her at home and encouraged her to make an appointment to see Dr. William Thayer, a world-renowned marriage and family therapist.

Gabrielle knitted her brows as she eyed Vivian while sitting cross-legged in the middle of the bed. "A therapist? You're kidding, right?"

Vivian moved from the foot of the bed to sit near Gabrielle. "No. I'm not kidding. You are going through a serious life-changing situation," Vivian said in all seriousness as she looked at Gabrielle's bedraggled appearance. "You are going to need help to get through this."

Although Vivian would not say it out aloud, she had a few anxious moments when she'd called and Gabrielle did not immediately respond. She tried to visit Gabrielle as often as she could but the more she listened to her, the more she was convinced that Gabrielle needed professional help. She was so concerned that she assigned each member of their prayer circle at church to pray with Gabrielle in the nights.

Gabrielle shifted position on the bed to lie back against the pillows. "I have you," she insisted. "I don't need a therapist. What would people think?"

Vivian saw the stubborn look on her face and knew that it was pointless to continue the conversation. "Promise me you'll pray about it," Vivian said quietly.

Gabrielle did not even pretend to respond.

But two days later, she cried all night and the following day she had to call in sick at work. Vivian mentioned seeing Dr. Thayer, again, and she garnered the courage to call and schedule an appointment, taking comfort in the fact that Dr. Thayer was a faith-based therapist.

For three months, she attended weekly meetings with Dr. Thayer then every two weeks and now monthly, when she felt the need.

At first, she had a difficult time expressing her feelings to Dr. Thayer because she had been raised by her now deceased mother, to keep a tight rein on her emotions - to be gracious, proper, and forgiving. Forgiving of everyone...but herself.

As time progressed, she worked through her infidelity issues which resulted from low self-esteem. She was surprised when Dr. Thayer made this assertion, because while she was not overly confident, she didn't deem herself to be a person with low self-esteem. So, she denied it and cried like a new born baby. However, when good sense prevailed, she agreed with Dr. Thayer.

Her low self-esteem was latent, buried deep in her psyche - the feeling of isolation, self-doubt, suppressed anger and shame - from not knowing her father and growing up with a strict mother. Further, her childhood experiences had not engendered a sense of confidence and she'd received very little positive reinforcement growing up, causing her to question her worth.

For sure her childhood, while marked by privilege in some respect, was not particularly happy. Her mother made it obvious that single parenting was not the lifestyle she'd dreamed of living. And when Gabrielle's innocence was stripped away, that further complicated her relationship with her mother.

Gabrielle's attempts to ask her mother about her father were spurned. Her mother was tight-lipped, giving away nothing. But, when Gabrielle was ten years old, her mother told her that her father was dead. Apparently dead to her. Because during Gabrielle's pregnancy, she had learned through Aunt Jean, who swore her to secrecy, that her father could very well be alive.

According to Aunt Jean, 'It was all very hush-hush from day one.'

Gabrielle's mother was caught up in a whirlwind romance with Joshua Lather, a journalist, whom she met on a cruise. They had gotten married in a quiet ceremony, and stayed married for about three months. One day, he left home on a work assignment and did not return. It was after that, that Paulina Lather found out she was pregnant.

While Gabrielle could freely talk with Dr. Thayer about the humiliation of not knowing her father and her emotionally crippling and torrid relationship with her mother, the process leading to forgiving a childhood friend was grueling. She didn't realize how much she hated him.

He had raped her.

Just mentioning his name to Dr. Thayer made her angry, leaving her emotionally drained. "It was not yours to take," she had screamed during that same therapy session. But, she couldn't bring herself to talk about it that day. Jesse Lowery had taken from her that which was precious and caused her to put up walls, walls that had locked her in…confined her, tortured her, and made her heart impenetrable.

During another session, Dr. Thayer picked up on her hints that she was ready to disclose what had happened on the day she was raped.

"Are you sure?" Dr. Thayer had asked, wanting to make sure she was fully prepared.

"Yes. I am," Gabrielle stated boldly, sitting cross-legged on a huge light blue chair across from him.

She had not spoken in details to anyone about being raped, not even Vivian. But today, she was ready to lay all the cards on the table. Thanks in part to the tremendous support and prayers of Vivian and the other four spirit-filled ladies in her prayer circle. She could not ask for more from them. Indescribable 'round the clock' support any time she needed it.

Gabrielle looked at Dr. Thayer realizing he was waiting for her to speak. She drew in a long breath preparing for the lengthy dialogue she knew she simply must have. It was time to shatter the darkness that had invaded her soul and kept her captive for so long.

"I was raped about twenty years ago at my cousin's wedding at the Zunicine Guest House and Villa, just an hour from where we lived back then. Ramona was only four years older than me, but she insisted on marrying Dawson Corbin, the love of her life. And Aunt Jean allowed it. Aunt Jeanette is my mother's sister," she filled in. "Of course Aunt Jean had to allow it. What else was she to do when her only child kept nagging her night and day, seeking her permission to marry Dawson? Not that she needed it." Gabrielle smiled slightly. "We all loved, Dawson. Still do. He is just a great guy."

She sighed burrowing deeper in the chair. "I had visited the Guesthouse with Ramona and her friends while they were making wedding arrangements so I was looking forward to her wedding day. The wedding took place in a magnificent hall, offering a breathtaking view of the beautiful garden surrounding the serene lake. Just stunning!" she emphasized. "In the distance, mountain peaks played peek-a-boo with the white smudges of silky clouds against the pale blue sky. A perfect, perfect place for a wedding. I couldn't imagine anywhere better."

Gabrielle paused, shifting her position on the chair.

"I had just turned sixteen, feeling all grown-up and confident." A slight smile played on her lips. "I felt elegant and soooo beautiful in my ivory sleeveless chiffon floor length gown. I couldn't wait to wear the dress. My mother had made it for me."

She jerked upright on the chair and looked Dr. Thayer in the eye. "Jesse Lowery had expressed an interest in me but I told him that I was not allowed to have a boyfriend. He said that he was okay with us remaining just friends. He lived next door so our platonic relationship was easy. Some days, we went to school and church together and he never gave me a reason not to trust him."

She turned on her side, curling her knees upwards until she was almost in a fetal position. "On the day of the wedding, I was outside the Guesthouse chatting with Allison, Jesse's older sister, when Jesse quietly signaled with his hand for me to follow him. I thought nothing of it. As soon as I could get away from my conversation with

Allison, I moved towards the entrance door to the Guesthouse, since that was where Jesse headed. He was waiting by the door. He grabbed my hand and we ran down the hallway. I remembered my evening slippers making clicky-clocking sounds on the ceramic tiles as we ran, giggling and making faces at each other."

Gabrielle sat up on the chair, staring blindly as her mind suddenly dared her to resurrect and speak of the vivid undesirable images of her sexual assault. Overwhelming fear gripped her heart, and in that moment, she wanted to remain in her captive state. But, she put an end to her thoughts and fought on, remembering the scripture, *"For God hath not given us the spirit of fear; but of power, and of love, and of a sound mind."*

"Do you need a break?" Dr. Thayer asked, sensing her dilemma.

"No. I'm fine," she responded quietly, before continuing with her saga. "We entered a room and Jesse quickly slammed the door and pressed me against it. And before I could speak, he pushed his tongue into my mouth. I tried desperately, desperately to get away from him. But, he would have none of it. In a rage, he threw me on the bed then straddled me. I struggled and writhed beneath his body, fighting as hard as I could, especially when his hand moved up my thigh. My heart began to hammer even louder when I heard my underwear snap as he yanked it from my body."

Gabrielle ran her hands across her face.

"I begged him to stop. Pleaded with him. But he covered my mouth with his hand, telling me, 'Shush! You've been begging for this all day.' Then, he grabbed my hands, pinning them above my head while he burrowed between my legs. With his hand still shielding my mouth, he plundered my womanhood - dominating, discarding, and destroying everything in its path. And, I just laid there. Frozen. Paralyzed with fear."

A single tear rolled down Gabrielle's cheek. "No words can express the agony I had experienced," she whispered hoarsely, briefly closing her eyes. "You know what I thought? This must be what dying feels like."

"It's okay. Release it," Dr. Thayer said gently.

She sobbed quietly, before continuing. "He was so merciless. I prayed it would end. And, after what seemed like an eternity, he dozed off - still on top of me! It was then that I heard people calling out our names - his mother, his brother, his sister, and finally...my mother. I found it difficult to breathe, so my voice came out in a whimper as I called out, "Mommy, save me!" But Jesse heard me because he awoke and covered my mouth."

Feeling as if she was suffocating, Gabrielle sprung out of the chair and walked to the large window covered by stylish royal blue drapes. She hesitated before parting the drapes, recalling that the day was muggy. But, she was pleasantly surprised to discover that the heavy rain had stopped, and replaced by a pretty blue sky and the promised sunshine.

She swallowed hard, closing her eyes for a moment as she struggled to find the courage to speak. "It was not over," she said quietly, her back to Dr. Thayer. "He had to get another filling."

She pressed one hand against the cool windowpane, mentally determining to break free as tears trickle down her face. "He hammered me, again and again; even though I was hollering out in pain. He insisted I tell him that I loved him. And when I wouldn't, he muttered, 'Don't fight this. I love you,' and then buried himself even deeper."

She pushed out a deep breath and wiped her eyes with her sleeve, then turned to face Dr. Thayer. "The room started to swirl around me so I squeezed my eyes shut. I drifted in and out of consciousness, thinking I was having a second near death experience. Finally, it was over and he rolled off me and pulled on his pants, while telling me to 'Clean up. Bathroom to the right.' Then, he disappeared through the room door. I could barely move but I walked as quickly as I could to the bathroom and locked the door, fearing he might return. After I cleaned up, I went back to the room and realized the comforter was a mess so I hauled it off the bed and washed the areas that were stained. I took the comforter back to the room and spread it over a two-seater leather sofa that was in the small lounge area."

She shook her head, a sardonic smile curving her lips. "After that, I slipped out of the room, and what do you know - I came face to face with my mother. Of course I was shocked to see her and she realized. She stared at me suspiciously for what seemed like forever."

Gabrielle returned to the chair and took a sip of her bottled water that was resting on the small table next to her chair. "I steeled myself as Mom opened the door, glanced in the room, and then inquired, 'Where were you?' Honestly, I didn't want to disappoint her so I told her I was exploring." Mom fell silent and through clenched teeth, she said, 'Let's go home.' Those were the last words my mother uttered to me for the next three weeks."

Gabrielle clasped her hands under her chin. "After that incident, my relationship with my mother was never the same. Paulina Lather simply ignored me…literally avoided me, her sixteen year old daughter. She didn't ask me anything about that day. I often caught her looking at me with disgust and disappointment. And each time, my heart just broke into several pieces."

Her bottom lip quivered uncontrollably as the horrible memory of her childhood assailed her and before long she let out a loud wail. "Why didn't she ask if Jesse had hurt me? She must have known." She covered her face with her hands, sobbing.

"Let's take a break?" Dr. Thayer said caringly.

"No. I'm alright," Gabrielle said, staring into space. "About six weeks after I was raped, I found out I was pregnant." She got up and walked to the window again and stared out motionlessly. "Lord, help me", she muttered, turning to put her back against the wall near the window, before looking at Dr. Thayer. "That was the worst news I could have heard. I collapsed in the bathroom at home. When I woke up, I hoped it was just a nightmare. But, it wasn't. I was pregnant."

Tears burned her eyes. "Thankfully Vivian, my friend was with me, because I became disoriented. And as if things could not have gotten any worst, I had to tell my mother. Far be it for Mom to ask questions, or extend any sympathy my way; she only expressed unbearable animosity towards me with each passing day."

Gabrielle wrapped her hands around her body as she began to shiver. "I wrote Mom a four page letter apologizing, but she did not respond. Mom died in a car accident," she concluded, "and we never spoke about what had happened to me."

She paused and was surprised to find herself breathing easier. Telling her childhood ordeal left her winded but a ton had been lifted from her delicate shoulder and she was no longer frightened. In fact, she was feeling rather relieved, peaceful and...expectant. She was determined to create a scene of triumph from the desecration of her childhood innocence.

"Would you like to stop for a while?" Dr. Thayer asked.

"Yes, please."

******

61

When the session resumed the following day, Dr. Thayer helped her to put her childhood events in perspective and gave her homework that would strengthen her resilience and courage. That day, they had also discussed the healing power of forgiveness.

Not that she needed any schooling about forgiveness.

She knew what the bible stated concerning forgiveness. She had even underlined St. Matthew 6:14-15, "For if you forgive men their trespasses, your heavenly Father will also forgive you. But if you do not forgive men their trespasses, neither will your Father forgive your trespasses." And, she'd learned forgiveness was a choice, a choice that she needed to make in obedience to God's word. A choice she had to make to heal the deep wounds of her past and to release herself into her next level of unprecedented success.

In the end, she did what was difficult but right.

She forgave Jesse Lowery and Larry Kanate. And, her mother.

By her last session with Dr. Thayer, she had developed self-compassion and a stronger sense of self. And eventually, she found the courage to forgive herself.

CHAPTER 6

STILL I RISE

"Wife, I did not know you had it in you," Quincy announced chuckling, as he dropped the last bag on the floor in the living room. "Do we have any money left in the bank?" They had just come home from shopping at the Macy's One Day Sale.

"Oh behave, Quincy!" Janie grinned, hitting him lightly on the arm. "It's a good thing I am not sensi-tive." She waved at the mountain of bags that Quincy and Blake had taken from the car. "I needed more stuff but I was frugal. Plus, half of these belong to Blake."

"Really?" Blake laughed out, removing his two bags from the pile. "I feel the love. I'll be in my room."

"We'll take the rest of your bags to your room," Janie hollered at his back. "That's love."

Blake stopped and turned to face a smiling Janie. "Q, get your wife!" he said shaking his head.

Quincy couldn't help but laugh at the happy banter between his wife and Blake. "I'm going to try but I don't want to come between love."

A smile crept up Blake's face and he winked playfully at Janie. "Yes, don't come between love," he stated in a deep dramatic voice. The sound of Janie giggling followed Blake as he disappeared down the passageway.

Half an hour later, Janie's screams of joy erupted from the living room and Blake left his room to investigate the reason for her loud display of happiness.

"Did I miss Christmas?" he asked jokingly when he saw Quincy and Janie in a warm embrace.

"Oh Blake, my Quincy is the best husband in the world." Janie smiled at Blake. "You know we didn't want children, but since last year I've been feeling the knocking of motherhood so I asked my dear husband to let us consider adoption." She looked lovingly at Quincy. "It certainly took him a while, but with prayer and plenty of nagging." She clapped her hands joyfully. "He has agreed to let us start the adoption process."

"Congrats!" Blake hugged her then slapped Quincy on the back. "Way to go. This is great news!"

"Yes." Quincy smiled widely. "We're about to add to the family. Whoot! Whoot!" He danced about then twirled Janie.

"Get ready, Uncle Blake," Janie grinned at him.

"I'm ready." Blake smiled happily at them. "I am excited. Mom and Dad will be excited too. At last, the possibility of a grandchild. Gabby and I had promised them..." he paused, when he realized what he was about to say. "So happy for you guys. We'll all be happy."

"Blake, I'm sorry," Janie said, looking at the vulnerability in his gaze. "I didn't mean to-"

"It's okay." Blake told her, pulling himself to full height. He didn't need her looking at him as if he was some tender basket case, frail nerves and all. "You'll make great parents."

"Thanks, Bro," Quincy said, and Janie smiled happily, adding, "Thanks!"

A few minutes later, Blake sat on the sofa near the window in his bedroom. He wanted to kick himself for showing vulnerability which he thought may have rained a little on Quincy and Janie's celebration. He ran a hand through his already disheveled hair, and reminded himself, *you've come a long way.*

A deep sigh left him as he recalled his emergency session with Bishop Clandon a month after he came back from Kansas. *Yep, that was me being vulnerable.* Instead of driving to Bishop Clandon's office, he had donned sweats and running shoes to take the trek to the church. Sweat ran down his face and back as he poured out his frustration on the sidewalk.

Forty five minutes later, he plopped down on a chair in Bishop Clandon's office, covering his face with both hands. He never remembered ever feeling this vulnerable, fearful, terrified, and uncertain about life.

"It's going to be alright, Son," Bishop Clandon told him, patting his shoulder as he wept.

"Why did she do this to us?" he muttered over and over again, when he was able to speak. "I gave her everything I had. Everything. Now, I have nothing." He wept inconsolably.

Bishop Clandon cradled his shoulder, praying, then told him, "I know it hurts but I know that God is going to take you through this."

Blake slumped back in the chair, attempting to pull himself together. "You know what, Bishop," he wiped his eyes with the back of his hands," I felt I had an opportunity to be a part of the winning team," he paused and stared blindly, "a part of a team that would be successful, come what may."

"Son, the victory is still yours. Life presents challenges to us sometimes, but I know that God is going to turn this situation around for your good."

Blake looked guiltily at Bishop Clandon who had returned to his seat behind the desk. "I have to admit, it did cross my mind to hurt Gabby the same way she hurt me. I wanted her to pay," he stopped and let out a tight breath, "to feel the pain that I...am feeling. But, I know too much to do something like that. The Spirit of the Lord kept telling me, 'You are not that kind of a person. You are better than this.'"

Bishop Clandon nodded in agreement, sending up a silent, *Thank you, Lord.*

A brooding expression covered Blake's face. "A part of me wants not to forgive her. I know I should, but I just cannot...forgive her. She..." he paused, gathering himself, "ripped out my heart, and then crushed it under her feet as if it was nothing."

Bishop Clandon shifted his eyes to avoid the pain he saw in Blake's eyes. He had seen many grown men in terrible anguish but none affected him this way. It was like his son was hurting. He remarked, "As you know, forgiveness is a choice...a decision you will have to make. Son, forgiveness is not an attribute of the weak; it's an attribute of the strong."

"I know it's the right thing to do, but, how do I come up with the strength to forgive her?"

"Only God can give you that strength. When you are ready, the Holy Spirit will help you. Blake, don't let this wilderness experience consume you. Instead, use this situation to dig deeper into God. Lay this situation at Jesus' feet; you cannot carry this burden."

A single tear rolled down Blake's cheek. "I feel betrayed...embarrassed...ashamed. I really ought to leave town for good," he confessed, hanging his head.

"That too will pass. I know the situation looks terrible and the future looks uncertain, but God is able to deal with the issues of your life. He is never challenged by the issues of our lives. I suggest you lay all those emotions at the feet of Jesus. If you constantly replay the negative then your situation will grow, take root in your heart and become an unbearable destructive force in your life. The favor of God is with you. So, shift your mind, shift your emotion, and let the Master go to work in you. He's a present help in times of trouble."

Blake nodded. He knew that Bishop Clandon was right.

That day, he released the anger he felt towards Gabrielle and forgave her.

A knock on his bedroom door took Blake back to the present.

"Come in," he answered.

Quincy entered and closed the door behind him. "Just checking on you," he said, taking a seat on the edge of the bed.

"I'm good, Q."

"Was thinking, have you heard Gabrielle's side of the story?"

Blake let out an exasperated sigh. "You think, I'm going to sit and listen to my wife tell me what she has done with another man? No. But, thanks for asking."

"Not like that, Bro. I doubt she would want to go into that. But I think you owe it to yourself to hear her out. It would be good for you to hear her side of the story and for you to express to her, how you feel about the situation."

A hollow laugh left Blake. "I already heard her side. She slept with Kanate. Is there more?"

Quincy looked at Blake. "Think about it. There's got to be more. The Gabrielle you know would never do something like this."

"Well, I hope she has resolved her issues so she won't destroy her next relationship."

Quincy's heart sagged at the thought of Blake divorcing Gabrielle. "Are you filing for a divorce?" he asked.

"No. I haven't made any decision yet regarding my relationship with Gabby. I'm asking the Lord how to proceed in that area." He wiped his face with both hands. "Right now, I'm focusing on finding an apartment."

Quincy smiled when he spotted the wedding band on Blake's finger. "Okay," he said rising from the bed and heading to the door. "I'll be praying too." A man of principles was how many referred to Blake because love undergirded everything that he did.

"Thanks."

When Quincy closed the door behind him, Blake closed his eyes and reclined deeper in the chair. He knew Quincy was rooting for Gabrielle, yet it didn't bother him. Quincy had always loved Gabrielle and she loved him right back.

Once again, his mind rested on Gabrielle. *I wonder if she's okay.* He'd skimmed the congregation for her last Sunday but could not find her. *Better watch yourself or you'll be rooting for her too*, he scolded himself, as he reached over the side of the sofa for his Bible that was resting on top of his laptop on the floor.

CHAPTER 7

SWEET SENSATIONS

Gabrielle scanned the parking lot at church. Last Sunday, she deliberately missed church. Her nerves were still frayed when thoughts of facing Blake assailed her. She knew she was being a coward but she just couldn't shake off the peculiar emotions that threatened to envelop her when she came in contact with Blake. Vivian had called, trying to persuade her to come on out but it was like 'flogging a dead horse.' But this Sunday was different. She'd decided to stop the foolish behavior.

All week she had prayed for strength and had also encouraged herself through, "…psalms and hymns and spiritual songs, singing and making melody in her heart to the Lord." She was made for worship and she was ready to worship God and…she was prepared to meet Blake, face to face.

The air felt comfortably cool when she hopped out of her car. Straightening her pretty coral lace sheath dress, she made her way to the entrance of the foyer. The plan was to take up her usual spot in the middle of the sanctuary and make contact with Blake after church. Her conversation with him wouldn't be intense, just conversational. She would find out how he was doing. Perhaps, how work was going. And definitely, she wanted him to know, she missed him, missed him deeply. *Ah, maybe I shouldn't say deeply. Sounds desperate. Stalkerish,* she mused.

Still deep in thought, she reached for the door handle to the foyer but before she could hold it, the door swung open and she collided with a hard male body.

"Ouch!" she gasped, her purse falling to the ground as she gripped his shirt to maintain her balance. "So sorry,

I-" The words died on her lips when she inhaled Blake's all too familiar scent.

His strong arms circled her waist to steady her. "Sorry," he murmured above her head. "Didn't know you were there."

She opened her mouth to speak, but no words came out. Overwhelmed, her body trembled as the aroma of his intoxicating cologne filled her nostrils.

"You're shaking," he remarked, one hand still circling her waist.

Before she could formulate a response, a female voice called out teasingly, "Get a room."

They glanced around to see Deacon Benjamin Solomon and Sonia, his wife, grinning at them. Sonia was a member of Gabrielle's prayer circle.

"Good morning, People of God," Blake greeted them, releasing a hearty laugh as he ushered Gabrielle away from the door.

Gabrielle smiled, attempting not to look self-conscious with Blake's arms still draped around her waist. She had almost stopped breathing. The months of not seeing him had done nothing to diminish her physical response to him.

"Good to see both of you," Deacon Solomon said, smiling as he opened the door for his wife, who winked at Gabrielle before slipping into the foyer.

"You too," Blake said, while Gabrielle smiled vaguely, desperately attempting to regain her composure.

"See you later," Deacon Solomon said, before slipping through the door.

"Okay," Blake responded before giving Gabrielle his full attention. "Are you okay?"

Gabrielle's eyes turned downward as she attempted to gracefully detach herself from him, a degree of awkwardness in her movements. "Blake, I'm..." It all felt strange - saying his name and standing so close to him. Yet, it was comfortable and right at the same time - the warmth of his touch and the care in his voice.

She smiled. *Haven't felt this way in a long time.* Yes, she missed him alright…all of him. She lifted warm eyes to his, and instantly stiffened as the nothingness in his gaze assaulted her senses. Her rosy thoughts vanished like pixie dust. She just had to take a second look. Yes. She was right the first time. Absolutely, no display of emotion. Nothing. Just distant.

The look was almost foreign to her after being subjected to his loving nature for so many years. And, there was also a glint of something else in his eyes.

Anger?

Scorn?

Judgment?

She stretched her senses but just couldn't quite put her finger on it.

What did I expect? A drum roll! She forced a lump down her throat then stepped further away from him and returned to her usual poised demeanor. "I'm good."

He knew his impassive look had unnerved her. *Good!* He had no intention of making it easy for her. He bent down to retrieve her purse, and then handed it to her. "Hope nothing broke."

"I doubt it." She took her purse from him, his casual manner causing the hair at the back of her neck to stand on end. "Thanks."

"You sure you're okay?"

As if you care! "Yes," Gabrielle insisted, slight annoyance lacing her voice.

Disbelief lit his eyes, but she refused to let him see how absolutely floored she was at his nonchalant behavior towards her. "I'll be in the sanctuary," she puffed out. Then, placing one foot before the other, she made her way to the door and yanked it open. Without a backward glance, she crossed the foyer, and entered the restroom. Her hands were shaking by the time she locked herself in one of the cubicles. *Breathe*, she told herself, mentally asking the Lord for strength.

Blake watched as Gabrielle walked away and in the midst of his mind pulling up the sordid details of what she had done to him, something hit him forcefully. *She was still gorgeous*. The moment the thought hit, annoyance spread across his face. Abruptly, he all but marched towards his car, mentally slapping himself that the thought even crossed his mind. But, his annoyance disappeared in an instant and his easy smile returned. He relaxed his tensed muscles. After all, he had progressed beyond her.

A few minutes later, Gabrielle entered the sanctuary, thankful that Blake was nowhere in sight. She took up her seat in her regular spot in the middle of the sanctuary. The service started out with thunderous praise and worship, which was great as usual. It was more like a celebration. The sanctuary was filled with shouts of joy as people openly worshipped God.

During the announcements, a nagging feeling of sadness descended on her and tears welled up as accusing voices flooded her mind. *It's your fault Blake is no longer on the Praise and Worship team. It is because of you and your selfish behavior that he is no longer singing to bless others. You destroyed his ministry.* Guilt ricocheted through her and she looked around wildly for a way of escape.

Deciding she did not want to disturb the others who were seated on the row, she held her peace, reminding herself to stay focused. But, she was glad when the moderator asked the congregation to take up comfortable spots for prayer time. She got on her knees before her seat, bowed her head and closed her eyes, than began to pray quietly. Tears flowed and her breaths labored as she confessed her thoughts to the Lord. Her prayer rose in fervor as she prayed for Blake, asking God to restore him to his ministry.

Soon, she sat listening to Bishop Clandon delivering a timely message titled, "I will not be hindered," that was relevant to daily living.

"God's purpose for our lives is not without hindrances," Bishop Clandon stated. "But, once we understand that God has destined us for purpose, we will press through the hindrances, be they external hindrances or internal hindrances."

Bishop Clandon walked from the altar and stood near the front pews as he made his point. "You must learn to overcome the hindrances that life will throw at you." He placed his hand on his chest. "I will not be hindered by myself or by my surroundings. I will not be hindered from accomplishing what God has designed for me to do."

Half an hour later, Gabrielle greeted a few persons as she made her way down the aisle. Out of the corner of her eyes, she saw frantic movements. When she glanced over, she saw Sister Clandon waving to get her attention. Gabrielle smiled at her.

"Need to see you," Sister Clandon mouthed, motioning with her hands for Gabrielle to wait somewhere as she made her way across the pews.

Gabrielle nodded then drifted to the nearest pew and stood, waiting.

She liked Sister Clandon - the high energy, confident, mother to three wonderful grown children, and an anointed singer. Although she only stood five feet four inches, Sister Clandon was known for her no-nonsense personality. Yet, she was not offensive. She spoke straight from her heart.

"Looking great, dear lady!" Sister Clandon greeted Gabrielle with a hug.

"Thank you. Right back at you." Gabrielle smiled at her, taking in her fitted, champagne and brown textured skirt suit.

"Thanks, dear," Sister Clandon returned her smile. "I wanted to give you this manual. It's one of the Sunday School Instructor's Guide that I would like for you to begin to browse. I want you to be equipped when you are back to teaching your Sunday school class."

"Oh. Okay." Gabrielle took the book from Sister Clandon. "Thanks."

Sister Clandon frowned at Gabrielle's puzzled look. "The Lord is working it out. I know He is." She grinned at Gabrielle. "Plus, you can't be on a break forever."

"Thank you. I do miss the kids."

"I know you do." Sister Clandon hugged her. "Have a wonderful Sunday afternoon."

Gabrielle hugged her tightly. "You too."

By the time Gabrielle exited through the foyer, there were few persons still milling about the church grounds. Her eyes darted around in search of Blake but there was no sign of him. Disappointed he'd already left, she shrugged her shoulders then rummaged through her purse for her car keys. Nearing her car, she looked towards the far corner of the parking lot where she'd seen him park his car two Sundays ago, but the spot was empty. "Oh well," she murmured, opening the car door and placing her Bible and the Sunday school manual on the back seat. *Why would he wait anyway?* She chided herself. *Have you forgotten the judgment in his eyes?*

Blake watched as Gabrielle approached her car. His eyes glued to her every movement. Unexpectedly, his heart fluttered and he stilled himself. She was beautiful...amazingly beautiful. Strands of her dark brown hair gently streamed behind her from the slight wind that was blowing. Her hair seemed longer than he'd recalled and he wondered if it was still as soft as he'd remembered. He lifted his hand to wave at her but she was absorbed in her thoughts so he waited until she was near. "Finally. Thought I was going to wait here forever," he said. His voice was devoid of emotion.

Gabrielle literally jumped at the sound of his voice. She was so caught up in her thoughts that she did not see him standing next to the tree near her car.

"Blake, what..." her voice sounded strangely high, "I-I didn't know you were waiting," she stammered, trying to ignore the anxieties that usually overtook her whenever she saw him.

He covered the space between them and stood gazing at her. "I know you didn't," he said quietly. He was not even sure why he waited for her. Was it habit or something else? Though he wouldn't acknowledge it, he was a little astonished by the warmth that tingled through his body when they had collided earlier that morning. There was no point in even acknowledging it; he was not going down that road again. "Is everything going well at home?" he asked purposefully. "Do you need anything?"

"All is well," she told him, disappointment seeping through her. *Is that all you're concerned about? Our home?*

"Okay. Great," Blake said. His posture indicated he was ready to go.

She eyed him. *Now would be a great time to be brave.* She put on a courageous smile before looking away. "Your presence is greatly missed at home."

She hated the slight tremor in her voice. It made her sound weak...and needy. But then, sounding needy may not be a terrible thing because she needed him to come home.

Home? Blake had to shut down the hollow laugh that almost escaped from his mouth, before attempting to formulate a response.

In her estimation, the awkward silence went on far too long. "Okay. Let me get out of here," she filled in, her bravery fizzling.

She stepped into the space between them and reached for the front door handle. But, before she could hold it, he gripped it, causing her hand to slide over his hand. She heard his sharp intake of breath and quickly removed her hand as sweet sensations rocked her body.

Instantly, heat infused her face. "So-sorry," she stammered, wanting to, but yet afraid to relish his nearness. Holding her breath, she waited for him to open the door, praying that her legs would not buckle. *Open the door,* she pleaded mentally, squashing herself against the car in an attempt to stifle all her longings. She could feel her body rebelling against the restraint of the moment.

Blake tensed at the feathery brush of her hand. He did not even realize he'd sucked in his breath until he was slowly releasing it. The door handle felt warm in his hand. She never failed to stir him…something he hadn't felt in a long while. Now, the slight spark inside him threatened to flare into a bonfire. He could feel the tautness in his body, the effort of holding back from the desire to pull her into his arms.

Suddenly, his nostrils flared. *What is this?* He checked himself mentally. How could his own body betray him? Surely, he should reject any emotional attachment to her. His feelings toward her were supposed to be dead. They died the day he found out she'd slept with another man. Annoyed, he pulled the door open for her.

Gabrielle ducked behind the steering wheel. She did not look at him…didn't want to any more. Not at the slight scorn and irritation in his eyes. Not at his controlled self-righteous anger, even though well-deserved. "Thank you," she said breathlessly.

"You're welcome," he responded, closing the door. And with a determined gaze, he headed to his car in the adjoining parking lot.

She let out a shallow breath before turning the key in the ignition. *Not as brave as I should have been, but that's a start.* She decided to take a peek at Blake, then felt herself gulp as she saw Zoe Thurman standing in his personal space, batting her eyes and trying to dazzle him with her brightest smile.

She wanted to slap the smile off Zoe's face. Everyone knew she was looking for a father for her two preteen boys. She'd heard that Zoe had taken a liking to Blake from the first day she had laid eyes on him at church. Back then, Zoe had made her intentions clear to the other women who were vying for Blake's affection. Gabrielle just knew she must have heard rumors about their marriage and probably thought this was her opportunity to conquer Blake.

Gabrielle pursed her lips and her eyes fired disapproving shots at Blake, hoping he would turn towards her. But, whatever Zoe was saying, clearly caught his attention because he was grinning at her and together they walked towards her car.

Gabrielle glared at Zoe's back. "You brazen...!" she hissed, then grabbed her mouth. Shocked that such a word almost came from her lips. Her eyes brimmed with tears as a voice in her head mocked her. *Green with envy, huh? You know you had a good man before you committed the unforgivable. Sure looks like he's moving right along.* Tears threatened to run down her cheeks so she quickly pulled out of the parking lot.

From the corner of his eye, Blake caught sight of Gabrielle observing as he spoke with Zoe. He was unaware that his eyebrows had shot to the top of his forehead as he watched Gabrielle speed out of the parking lot. *She sure is in a hurry to get away. What's she up to now?* He relaxed his face and tried to focus on his conversation with Zoe.

CHAPTER 8

UNEXPECTED CONFESSION

Later that week, Blake stood back, hands on hips, to admire his handiwork, and he was considerably pleased as he looked at the beautiful flowers and bushy foliage in the garden that surrounded Quincy and Janie Montgomery's home. He had successfully cleaned out the unwanted shrubbery and watered the flowers and plants, then moved some of the house plants that had sojourned on the sunny back patio, indoors because of the cool fall weather.

Early spring after his separation from Gabrielle, the flowers were budding, and he had found comfort and peace in gazing through his bedroom window at the portion of the garden beneath the window. He had enjoyed seeing the daffodils, but he couldn't wait for the tulips and primroses to be in full bloom.

He used the back of his glove to brush away strands of hair that were pasted on his forehead before hauling the thick green, expandable garden hose towards him.

"Hey there!"

He turned towards the sound of Janie's voice and found her smiling at him from the back patio.

"You are hard at work I see," Quincy commented from Janie's side.

Blake smiled at them. "Hello, my people! Just doing a little something to occupy my-" He paused, distracted by the ringing of his cell phone. "Give me a minute, please," he told them, pulling the phone from his back pocket.

"Hey, Vivian! How are you?" Blake answered, as he wrapped up the hose.

"Doing great!" Vivian responded cheerfully. "How about you?"

"Doing well," Blake said, smiling. "I know I haven't responded to your email regarding helping out at our Family Life Conference but I will. I need to get with Bishop Clandon before I take on any assignments."

"Thanks, Blake. But, that's not why I am calling. Angelica would like to speak with you."

"Sure," Blake smiled. He was fond of Angelica, Vivian and her husband, James Moore's spirited nine-plus-going-on-thirty-year old daughter.

"Hello, Uncle Blake!" Angelica charmingly greeted him.

"Hello, my Earth Angel," Blake responded, sending her into fits of giggles.

"Uncle Blake, I know I've said it a thousand times but I love when you call me that. Just wonderful! Anyway, I miss you. I have seen Aunt Gabrielle a few times but not you." Then, she added in a suspicious tone. "Are you avoiding me?"

Blake couldn't help but chuckle. "Noooo, Earth Angel. You'll see me soon. I know your party is coming up."

"Oh great, Uncle Blake!" She let out a few girlish giggles. "Because that's why I'm calling, so glad you remembered. It's going to be a Barbie princess theme party," she informed him.

"Does that mean I have to dress up like Ken?" Blake grimaced.

Angelica burst out laughing. "Uncle Blake, no!" When she managed to get her laughter under control, she added, "Please, Uncle Blake, come as yourself."

"I sure will, Earth Angel."

"Thanks, Uncle Blake. I will see you soon."

"Okay. Have a good evening."

With that Angelica disconnected the call.

Blake smiled as he dropped his cell phone in his back pocket. *That child is older than her years.*

"Blake," Janie broke into his thoughts, beaming as she held on to one of the columns on the patio. "Those plants were literally dying because of lack of water. Thank you!"

"Anything for you, Janie." Blake smiled at her as he continued to wrap up the garden hose at the steps leading to the patio. "It's the least I could do for all you've done for me."

When his off-site afternoon meeting ended early at a smaller branch of Petrosa International Bank, he decided that he would take on the gardening project which Quincy had been promising Janie that they both would do one weekend. But truth be told, Quincy was not the outdoor type. However, he assisted his wife with gardening to appease her.

Janie shooed him off with her hands. "We are only too glad to have you."

"Yes," Quincy confirmed, reclining on a chair nearby.

Janie gazed at him then turned her attention back to Blake as he entered the patio. "I did ask someone who shall remain nameless to help me with the garden. He told me that with your help, Blake, it would be done in a jiffy. But, nooooo."

Quincy chuckled as he walked towards her. "Nameless? Is that how you see me?" He hugged her from behind. "Thought I was your darling."

"Yes, you are," Janie relented looking star-struck as Quincy lovingly kissed her cheek and whispered sweet nothings in her ear.

Blake shook his head at Janie. "I can't believe you're making it that easy for him."

She grinned back at Blake. "Please forgive me. This man has me all weak for him."

Blake chuckled as he walked by them to drop the hose in the far corner of the patio. "At least I know where your loyalty lies."

Janie giggled loudly as Quincy tickled her sides, then reeled out of his arms and ran towards the back door. "Behave," she said breathlessly, hanging onto the doorpost, "you are under punishment for not taking care of the garden."

A mischievous smile appeared on Quincy's face. "Punishment?" He walked slowly towards Janie, with no honorable intention.

"Yes. Punishment," she emphasized. She opened her arms. "And, don't let this white silk blouse fool you. I will show you no mercy."

"No mercy!" Quincy made a dash for her and she ran into the house, playfully screaming for help and it was no surprise that Quincy followed suit.

Blake stared out the back patio at nothing in particular. *Don't go there*, he admonished himself, attempting to ignore the tingle of jealousy that began to creep in his heart as he watched Quincy and Janie. He and Gabrielle used to be playful towards each other.

A few minutes later, Blake heard the patio door close and turned to see Quincy as he sat on a chair near the door. "Thanks, Man!" Quincy said to Blake. "You know I'm not the outdoor type."

Blake looked at him. "I know. You owe me one."

Quincy chuckled as Blake sat across from him. "Yes, I do! Don't be collecting anytime soon."

"We'll see about that," Blake smiled at him. Just then, his cell phone rang and he looked at the caller ID. "Let me take this," he told Quincy, reclining on the chair as he answered. "Hey, Zoe! What's up?"

"Pretty much everything!" Zoe responded, finding herself funny. "Thanks for dropping off the Kirk Franklin CD. Thought you were going to drop it off this evening when I'm home."

"I left work early today so I decided to just swing by and leave it under the front door mat."

Zoe let out a defeated sigh. "It's the second time that you are leaving a CD under the mat. Is being in my company that bad?"

"Come on, Zoe!" Blake chuckled. "You're okay!"

Zoe chuckled too. "Ah, there is the Blake I know. Remember, you promised to help me set up my computer as soon as it is delivered."

"Yes, I remember."

"Okay. Have a greaaaat evening!"

"Will do. You too." Blake smiled as he disconnected the call.

"Zoe Thurman, huh?" Quincy asked.

"Yep," Blake responded, reclining deeper on the chair, and stretching out his long legs.

"You may want to be careful with that one. Word on the street is that trouble follows her wherever she goes. You know she was attending our church before she moved on to yours."

"Nothing to be careful about," Blake replied. "I'm just helping her out." He knitted his eyebrows. "I'm still a married man." He always prided himself on living on the principles of God's words rather than emotions.

"Does that mean if you weren't married, you would be interested in Zoe?"

Blake looked at his brother sharply. "No. Like I said, I'm just helping her out."

"Don't be fooled, Bro. You may not be interested but a woman like Zoe only has one thing on her mind - to ensnare you into her web of deceit, and then spew you out if things don't go her way." Quincy chuckled. "Sooner or later, you'll find out Zoe only has one true love - herself. There is no room for anyone else." Laughter danced in his eyes, as he animatedly declared, "She's in love," and then motioning with his hands three times, he highlighted "with herself, and herself, and herself."

Blake's eyebrows rose in surprise. Under normal circumstances he would have found Quincy's dramatic abilities downright hilarious, but at that moment, his focus was on clarifying his association with Zoe. "I have no intention of building that kind of relationship with Zoe. But, you seem to know a lot about Zoe."

"Just a little. She tried her feminine wiles on me when I was trying to 'help her out,'" Quincy said, using his index fingers to emphasize the expression. "But, she really did a number on a friend of mine. So, just be careful."

"Always, Q," Blake responded.

A deep sigh of relief escaped Quincy. "Glad to hear you say that."

"I'm not looking for any more trouble than I already have."

Quincy gave him a long hard look, without saying a word.

"That's the truth," Blake confirmed. Suddenly, he felt peeved. "I hope you're not thinking I'm trying to get back at Gabby."

"Are you?"

"Look, Q, I'm not in the mood for this foolishness."

"Don't think this is easy for Gabrielle. She's hurt too."

Blake gulped, annoyance written all over his face. "Hurt? Man, did you say hurt?" Blake felt his blood boiling. "I'll tell you what being hurt is like." He leaned forward as he spoke. "It's like life has been sucked out of you at a moment when you least expect it," he rasped. "It's like falling and the weird thing is, you are aware that in any given moment you're going to hit the ground, and hit it hard. It's hoping, just hoping because you cannot pray, that you'll make it to the next day." Then, through clenched teeth, "Don't tell me what being hurt feels like."

Quincy stared at him quietly for a moment. Blake was annoyed. Hurt. Angry. And, rightly so. Sure he had every right to feel that way. His life had taken an unplanned detour. He still shuddered every time he thought about Blake's state of mind when he'd picked him up after the incident with Gabrielle. He was so concerned that he and Janie had taken leave from work so Blake wouldn't be alone.

The day after the incident, when lunch time came around and there was still no sign of Blake, he'd decided that it was time to put on his big brother hat. He took the soup Janie had prepared to the room that Blake occupied. There was no response to his knock on the door so he opened the door and found Blake wrapped round a pillow, looking completely devastated.

"Brought soup," Quincy said cheerfully, setting it on the nightstand, then slightly opening the curtains.

Blake's bloodshot eyes could barely focus. "Thanks," he murmured, his sadness morphing into despondency.

"Anytime," Quincy said. He was happy that Blake was at least responding.

Blake glanced around the room and felt like the walls were closing in. "Have you ever been blindsided, betrayed, and lied to, and then unexpectedly hit from every direction?" he asked, as Quincy stood at the foot of the bed looking at him. "Q, she destroyed my heart," he whispered, "right before my eyes."

That day, Quincy was extremely attentive, and he cried too - for more than one reason - as Blake shared a little about what had occurred between him and Gabrielle.

Blake stood up then plopped back down on the chair, which brought Quincy back to the present.

What man could stand to look at his wife if she cheated on him? Quincy thought, looking stealthily at Blake. Still, knowing what he knew, he just had to plead Gabrielle's case.

"Blake, I know you're hurting," Quincy told him frankly. "All I'm saying is that Gabrielle is hurting too."

Blake did not say a word, knowing he might speak words he would definitely regret.

Quincy was well aware of the anger flashing in Blake's eyes but he still wanted Blake to hear his heart. It was at that precise moment that he quietly made his confession. "I know Gabrielle is hurting, because I have been there too."

The unexpected confession jerked Blake out of his own problem. "What did you say?"

Quincy looked him in the eye. "I cheated on Janie."

Blake looked at Quincy, his mind reeling with questions.

"Sorry. I wanted to tell you but you had just started courting Gabrielle," Quincy said. "I didn't want to dampen your happiness."

Blake looked at Quincy, not sure how to react to the news of his infidelity. "Janie?"

"Yes. She knows," Quincy said. "She has forgiven my moment of weakness and I will spend my entire life, just being thankful to her for forgiving me, and giving me a second chance."

Blake regarded him keenly. *Moment of weakness? Isn't that what Gabrielle claimed she had when she slept with Larry Kanate? If I hear that term one more time, I will definitely be kicking something, something that I haven't already kicked.*

"I know you don't understand," Quincy stated humbly, "but, I'm asking you to listen."

Blake nodded.

"It happened five years ago, around the time of the accident." Quincy shook his head. "I had no intention of doing anything like that. Not with anyone, and of all persons, not with Julisa. She was the training manager for our Products Division. You know back then, I worked as the Production Director for Celworth Paper Products Company. Julisa and I had a professional relationship, strictly professional," Quincy emphasized. "It was a part of my job responsibility to proof her training documents for company products."

Blake looked at him. "So what happened?"

"A team of four of us left for Saint Paul, Minnesota to present our company offerings to a fortune 500 company. We were excited; it was a huge opportunity for Celworth. On the first day, after we settled in, we met for an early dinner at the restaurant in the hotel. After dinner, I wanted to see a little of the city and Julisa volunteered to accompany me."

Quincy tried to assess Blake's reaction. But there was nothing in his eyes. "We had a good time, nothing strange happened between us. Later that evening, I walked her to her room and I waited in the small lounge area in her room, for her to return with a few of the training documents I hadn't reviewed. When she returned, we briefly looked at the documents then chatted for a little about this and that."

Quincy lifted a hand to emphasize that their conversation was neither here nor there, before continuing, "At a point in our conversation, I remembered Julisa saying that she loves to dance." Quincy paused, before admitting, "I was surprised. Okay, I was absolutely taken aback and curiosity got the better of me because she didn't look like the type to dance. So, she volunteered to show me and to be honest, I did not know what to expect…the waltz, samba, ballet…" Quincy shook his head. "Bro, she asked me to recline deeper on the chair, and then she proceeded to give me a lap dance. At first, I was stunned, I couldn't move but once I got over the shock of it all, I started to enjoy the moment, and to make a long story short, we ended up making out." A deep sigh escaped Quincy; clearly, he had still not come to terms with his infidelity.

Blake remained quiet, numbed by the whole disclosure. In the extended silence, he glanced at Quincy.

"Please don't judge me," Quincy said, tears rolling down his cheeks. "To this day, I just can't believe I did such a vile thing. Sleeping with Julisa was the furthest thing from my mind when I left home that morning for Minnesota. The night it happened, I didn't sleep, not even a wink. I was in sheer agony over what I'd done. I was so out of it the next day on my way to the presentation that I caused the accident." He wiped his eyes with his sleeves. "I could have killed everyone in the car that day."

"Thank God, everyone escaped unhurt," Blake said quietly.

"I told Janie the night I returned home from Minnesota. You can well imagine her reaction 'cause you've been there. I lived in misery and pain through it all. It took us a while to get our lives back on track but Janie means the world to me and she knows it." He looked Blake in the eye. "I have never been in your shoes and I pray to God I will never be. But, I can tell you this - you can spend your entire life being bitter because challenges came at you that you didn't expect. That would be the easy part." Quincy paused, noting Blake's stubborn countenance. "But as long as you keep focusing on the hurt, the disappointment, the pain…you will never be able to grab ahold of the amazing future that God has for you."

Still no reaction came from Blake.

"You still love Gabrielle and she loves you. You have to find it in your heart to release her from the mistake she made and let go of the situation…for your sake, for the sake of your future."

Blake looked at the floor for a moment before meeting Quincy's eyes. "I have forgiven her but continuing our marriage is a no, no. Absolutely not!" A flash of pride lit his eyes. "Can't do it. Won't do it." He stared ahead of him at nothing in particular.

CHAPTER 9

NOT READY

"Thanks for checking on me, Q," Gabrielle smiled. "Have a great evening."

"Does that mean, you'll stop avoiding me, and my wife?" Quincy said in a formidable voice but she knew he was teasing her. "You are always welcome to visit us, anytime." He had decided to check up on Gabrielle the day after his confession to Blake.

"Q!" She couldn't help the giggles that erupted from her lips. "No such thing. I sure will."

"Denial, denial," he chuckled. "'The proof is in the pudding.'"

"I know I've been MIA but I promise to visit soon."

"I won't be holding my breath. Still, I'm grateful that you allowed me to have lunch with you. How long ago was that? Four months ago, but who's counting. Plus, you're still taking my calls. Yes. I am grateful."

"There, I'm not so bad then. We're still in touch. I promise I'll do better."

"And, I'm holding you to that promise," he insisted. "Talk with you soon."

"It's a deal. Don't forget to tell Janie I said hello. Bye," she responded, then disconnected the call.

Her lips curved in a gentle smile as she grabbed a cart at Talpher Supermarket near her workplace and headed for the aisle with canned soups.

"There you are. Let's see the calorie count," she muttered staring intently at the label on a bowl of microwaveable chicken noodle soup. She placed the bowl back on the shelf and moved a little further down the aisle to check out the other soups.

Counting calories was something she had not gotten into but recently the news had been filled with stories about food manufacturers putting unhealthy ingredients in processed foods. She was on the lookout for high percentages of sugar, sodium and, definitely trans-fat which increased bad cholesterol while lowering good cholesterol.

She was slowly returning to preparing a full meal in her kitchen at home. Since Blake left, she'd cut down on cooking because she was so accustomed to both of them cooking together, especially on Saturday afternoons. It was like couple's therapy - a time to chat, laugh, and play with each other.

She glanced at the time on her cell phone. She had time to burn before meeting Sister Clandon at church. She'd decided it didn't make sense to go home after work, since she had the meeting.

Suddenly, she felt odd, something was not quite right. Nervous, she glanced up the aisle only to find herself staring at Larry Kanate. Icy shock rocked her body and her mind shrieked several commands at the same time, but *run* was the loudest as she stood rooted to the spot, the color draining from her face. Scarcely able to breathe, she observed Larry talking to a woman whose back was turned towards her. She couldn't hear what he was saying to her, but his body language indicated that he was about to come down the aisle.

In an instant, her eyes met Larry's and Gabrielle felt some kind of subliminal exchange between them - a dialogue of sorts. He intended to speak with her. Recoiling, she shook her head at him, and heard an emphatic "no" coming from her lips. Her feet felt like lead weights as she swung her cart in the opposite direction. She hurried away towards the far corner of the supermarket, apprehensively glancing up each aisle. But, when she heard Larry yelling her name, she left her cart and bolted for the exit doors.

Her heart hammered as she quickly ran before a small group of shoppers in the parking lot. She looked behind her then sprinted to her car when she saw Larry at the entrance of Talpher, scanning the parking lot.

Phew! Gabrielle pulled out of the parking lot. *Lord, help me. Feeling like such a chicken but I'm not ready for a face to face with Larry.*

A few minutes later, Gabrielle pulled up in the church's parking lot. She closed her car door, happy to see a few other cars because she had a twenty-minute wait time for Sister Clandon.

She waved to two men who were doing lawn care before entering the sanctuary. There was no one in sight when she entered the sanctuary, but she heard inaudible voices coming from behind the doors that led to the altar.

She sat on the front pew and then closed her eyes. *I may have to meet with Larry one day because he seems to need closure…but now is definitely not the time.* Letting out a slow breath, she opened her eyes and her focus shifted to the golden hue on the altar. She watched as the brilliant yellow rays of the evening sunlight danced and sparkled languorously from the windows. She couldn't stop the smile that touched her lips for she'd often watched Blake fervently ministering in song on the altar before the congregation. She admired how he gave a hundred percent to all his commitments. With Blake, it was all in or not at all.

She remembered how excited he was about planning for their upcoming anniversary. "It's a surprise," he told her animatedly. The look in his eyes captivated her. It was that same smile that won her heart some five years ago.

Her eyes twinkled. *Love is a beautiful thing.*

They say love strikes anytime and anywhere, sometimes when you least expect it … in the grocery store, the mall, on the street…anywhere.

Turns out, they were right. Love strikes anytime and anywhere.

It was lunch time and she'd driven up to the church to collect Sunday school teaching resources from Sister Clandon. And, it was there that she saw Blake, rather heard him. She'd walked quickly to see the man behind the voice. He had the voice of an angel.

She yanked the handle of the front door to the foyer but it was locked so she ran to the side of the building and peeped through the window. Blood rushed to her cheeks when she saw him. Her heart skipped a beat… too many beats, and in that moment she felt all the air being sucked out of her lungs.

She'd gazed at him with forlorn, hopeful eyes craving his undivided attention. But, he didn't see her. He was oblivious of her presence. He didn't mean to. He was in the presence of God, in full blown worship, singing and making melody on the keyboard to the Lord.

A man of God! There was a stirring in her impenetrable heart.

Suddenly, he stopped. He knew he wasn't alone. His eyebrows furrowed; he felt her presence. She held her breath as he started walking towards her through the rays of sunlight, then his mouth tilted into a smile and he waved her towards the side door leading to the sanctuary.

"Hello there," he greeted her, his eyes zeroing in on her as she stood on the doorstep. "You must be, Gabrielle Lather." Her eyebrow lift asked him to explain. "I am Blake Montgomery, the new chief musician for the church. Sister Clandon told me to let you know that she had to run out, she'll be back shortly."

She smiled, noticing his distinct, handsome features as she extended her hand, saying, "Hi! Welcome."

His handshake was steady yet gentle, giving her the sense that he was self-assured and strong. But, the moment their hands touched, she fought against the way her pulse took an enormous leap and she had to resist the urge to snatch her hand away. There was a strange expression in his eyes, but she couldn't decide if it was because of the delicious sensations that occurred as their hands touched or if it was her frantic desire to remove her hand from his grasp.

After their handshake, she'd decided to wait in her car. A chuckle escaped her as she slid behind the driver's seat, trying to maintain her usual prim and proper decorum. She was unable to understand the effect he had on her, Miss I-have-it-all-together. It had been a long time since any man had captured her attention and evoked such a powerful, noticeable response from her. Still, she had to admit that the new chief musician, Blake Mont-something-of-the-sort was a fine looking creature. *And, why do I feel like a child with a lollipop*? Giggling foolishly, she mentally reminded herself that she was not a teenager but that she had recently celebrated her thirtieth birthday. *Feelings are just that...feelings.* She drew in a deep mind-clearing breath to dismiss the effect that the new chief musician had on her.

"Gabrielle!" Sister Clandon called out, jerking her out of her thoughts as she glided her elegant frame up the aisle towards Gabrielle.

"Hi, Sister Clandon!" Gabrielle rose and hugged her. "You look great!" Gabrielle said, admiring her medium-length wavy jet black hair and scoop neck purple dress that fell into a rippling high low hemline.

"Thanks, dear!" Sister Clandon beamed as they sat on the pew. "Trying to keep my husband on his toes. We have a date later."

"That's wonderful." Gabrielle grinned at her. "I'm sure Bishop Clandon will be dancing the evening away with you. This is a great outfit."

"Thanks!" Sister Clandon smiled at her. "So, how are you doing?"

Gabrielle pursed her lips. *How am I doing?*

Sister Clandon touched Gabrielle's hand. "It can't be that bad. Thought you were making great progress."

Gabrielle smiled at her. "Yes, I am. Actually, I'm doing great. Just praying that Blake will return home soon."

"Robert and I are praying for both of you," she encouraged. "Listen to the voice of truth and continue to press forward. God is faithful."

"Thank you," Gabrielle nodded in agreement. "Whenever fear cripples me, I have to remind myself the battle is the Lord's."

"Yes. That's it!" Sister Clandon agreed. ""Be strong in the Lord and in the power of His might.""

Gabrielle smiled at her. "I'm staying focused."

"Great!" Sister Clandon returned her smile, then handed her a package. "Here are the Sunday school students' training materials for you to go through. I am expecting the additional instructor's training manuals soon. Will let you know when I have them in hand."

"Okay. Great! Thanks so much! Have fun on your date."

Sister Clandon winked at her as they stood up. "You bet I will. Let me walk out with you. Robert is waiting in the car."

Gabrielle's eyes widened. "I'm sorry to have kept you. Didn't know Bishop was waiting."

Sister Clandon lifted a hand to halt Gabrielle's apology as they exited through the side door. "Not a problem."

Outside the building, Bishop Clandon was waiting in the car with the engine running. Gabrielle wanted to wave hello, but his head was bowed as if he was looking at something.

Sister Clandon hugged Gabrielle, and whispered, "The hotter the battle, the greater the anointing."

"Thank you," Gabrielle murmured.

Sister Clandon looked towards her husband and her face lit with mischief. "See you on Sunday. Let me get this show on the road."

"Alrighty!" Gabrielle grinned and walked in the opposite direction to her car. She placed the package with the Sunday school training materials on the passenger seat, just as her cell phone rang. She reached for it in the side pocket of her purse, waving to the Clandons as they drove away.

"Hey, Viv!" she answered.

"Gabs, just checking on my girl," Vivian beamed. "Passing by your home in another fifteen minutes and was going to swing by."

"That would be nice. I just picked up Sunday school training materials from Sister Clandon at church. I should be home shortly."

"Okay. I'll wait."

"Yes, please wait," Gabrielle said. "I just saw Larry."

Vivian sucked in her breath. "Really?"

"Oh, yes! See you in a few minutes."

Smiling, Gabrielle pulled out of the church yard. *Thanks to Viv. I will always know what it feels like to have someone in my corner.*

CHAPTER 10

A LOVE SO RARE

Two days later, Gabrielle decided to put action behind her prayers and words of faith.

It was twelve midnight when she made the call.

"Hello," Blake answered huskily, sounding half asleep.

Her pulse picked up speed at the sound of his voice. She'd always loved the sound of his voice when he woke from his slumber. The raspy, grating sound heightened her senses, creating delightful sensations in her stomach. And the pleasure was all hers when she woke beside him in the mornings. 'Good morning, beautiful!' he would say as he smiled gently at her. His smile was filled with love - rare, pure and absolutely enchanting love, which she'd grown accustomed to enjoying. No matter how many times she saw his smile, it made her blush. And, when she did recover, she would return his smile, and respond, 'Good morning, honey!' before dropping her head on his chest and hugging him tightly to breathe in his enduring love.

Should I wake him? She reasoned with herself and decided to press on. "Hi, Blake," she said softly, picturing his face.

"Hey, babes. What's up?" he responded.

She couldn't stop the smile that lit her face at his term of endearment. "Just wishing you a happy, happy birthday. I am praying the continued favor of God on your life. Have an amazing…"

Blake knitted his brows, then squinted and stared in the darkness. *Am I dreaming…about Gabby?* His heart quickened again at the sound of her silky voice and it was then he realized he was holding his cell phone to his ear.

"Gabby?" he asked propping up on his elbow.

"Yes, Blake." She heard the pause and figured he just came out of his slumber. "I was just wishing you a happy birthday. We usually stay up for-"

"Thanks," he cut her off. "I appreciate the gesture. Have a good night."

"Blake, you don't have to be rude," Gabrielle charged.

"Gabby, I'm not being rude. It's late and I have work in the morning."

You never had a problem staying up late before, she wanted to tell. But, she held her peace. "Okay," she said before disconnecting the call.

Infuriated, Blake fell back against the bed and groaned slightly. *What does she want from me? I'm trying to keep things between us as courteous as possible.* He closed his eyes briefly as he felt a poke in his heart. He just knew she would be crying herself to sleep. Now, he felt the need to call her back...against his will. Annoyance gripped him and he clenched the bed covers in his hands. *I'm not in the mood for this.*

Gabrielle's cell phone rang and she deliberated whether or not to answer. *Oh, my heart is wounded,* she lamented, tears streaming down her neck. She pulled back the bedcover from over her head to pick up the phone from her bed. It was Blake. She mopped her face wondering if she should answer, knowing that she could not handle the lack of warmth in his voice. Frustration creased her forehead. "Yes," she answered.

"Sorry," he said dryly, then decided to be kinder. "Sorry, if I came across as unappreciative. Thanks for the birthday wishes."

"You're welcome," she answered in a dull monotone.

"Is everything alright with you?"

"Yes."

"Gabby, I'm trying. Don't make the situation any harder."

No, he didn't! She wanted to stomp her feet and scream at him. *Harder? You don't have a clue what that means. Harder is you, not coming home. Harder is us not being a family. Harder is me not celebrating your birthday with you. Harder is me pretending that everything is okay when I am fading on the inside. Harder is me, trying to hold it together every time I look at you. So, puh-lease, Blake, don't talk to me about making the situation harder than it already is. Shoooot!*

But instead, she replied, "Okay, see you around. Have a good night."

"Thanks. You too."

Blake let out a huge sigh of relief as he laced his hands behind his neck on the bed. While he was never one to celebrate birthdays, during their courtship Gabrielle had gotten all worked up about it so he'd agreed that birthdays would be a time of celebration in their home.

So he was slightly annoyed last November when she had totally forgotten his birthday. They often laughed about it, dubbing it her "senior moment" because she had never admitted that she'd forgotten. He thought it very strange that she had not mentioned his birthday when she left for work that morning so he figured she had something big planned and was holding out on him. But when lunch time came and no call came from her, he knew that she'd forgotten. He attributed this to her hectic work schedule. He decided to call her and they chatted for a while then he reminded her. She could not help the loud gasp that emanated from her lips, but she quickly covered her track as he laughed and laughed some more. Later that day, they celebrated in grand style at an upscale restaurant, and then took the party home.

Blake knitted his brows still unable to comprehend why she would have cheated on him. *We had a great life together. The perfect couple, some said.* He wandered back in time, recalling how she had him gushing over her, even before he said, "Hello." The memory rapidly flooded his mind, peaked his senses and instantaneously his temperature soared.

Time seemingly stood still the first time he saw her through the window at the church. He'd heard a slight sound, glanced towards the window only to have his breath taken away at the sight of her long, dark brown hair lightly blowing in the wind. *She was gorgeous!* Her wide eye, I-am-so-embarrassed look as she gaped at him made him chuckle quietly...*just so priceless*. He walked towards her, flashed her a smile to ease her embarrassment, and then waved his hand towards the side door nearby.

"Hello there," he greeted her, hiding his amusement when he opened the door. "You must be, Gabrielle Lather." Her eyebrows shot up to her hairline and he explained. "I am Blake Montgomery, the new chief musician for the church. Sister Clandon told me to let you know that she had to run out, she'll be back shortly.

He watched her nervously push her hair behind her ear, before bashfully saying, "Hi! Welcome!" and extending her hand.

For no reason, he found himself smiling at her. "Thanks! Great meeting you!" he said.

As they shook hands, a surge of awareness hit him and he mentally checked himself, after all, he did not know her. He gazed at her hoping that she would say something else so he could observe her further. As he watched her, he noted his eyes were not playing a trick on him. *She is beautiful. God took the time to pull her cheekbones to just the right height to create her perfectly proportioned oval-shaped face.*

"I'll wait for Sister Clandon in my car," she told him.

"Okay." He watched her walk back to her car but not before noticing that the twinkle in her light brown eyes mesmerized him, stirring his vital signs. She definitely piqued his interest. There was something different about Gabrielle Lather, and he wanted to find that something.

He had made it his duty to greet her on Sundays and any other time that she was at church. And, he quickly found out that she was different alright - genuinely beautiful inside and out, despite her slightly hardened and prim deportment.

Four weeks later, he decided that he was going to be more direct with her to capture her attention. "You look great," he told her in the parking lot after a mid-week church meeting.

At his compliment, her chin rose along with her perfectly arched eyebrows and although there was a glimmer of appreciation in her eyes, he was sure he also saw a tinge of amusement. She was not sold on his overture.

"Thanks," she responded.

Her expression told him, she clearly was not about to fall all over him. Nope. Not like some of the other women at church who unashamedly showed and expressed their affection for him. Yes, her signal was clear. He knew he had to shift to a higher gear, because he needed her to understand the full extent of his interest in her.

Going forward, he doubled his efforts to engage her in conversations and took advantage of any opportunity to reach out to her but she still would not allow him in…always distant. Yet, although she hadn't encouraged his interest, several times, he had felt her gaze roaming in his direction when they were in the same space at church. And, on a few occasions, he caught her staring at him.

After two months of miserably failing to gain her affection, he decided to be forthright with her after Bible Study one Wednesday night. He waved her down when he saw her driving out of the parking lot.

"I would like to take you on a date," he told her, smiling confidently.

She was surprised and unprepared for his request and she nibbled on her lips for a moment. He could tell she was mentally assessing whether or not to take the plunge. Relief hit him when her expression changed to reflect a mild interest.

"I would like that," she responded quietly.

He could barely contain himself. "Great! Is Friday evening good?"

She nodded, pressing the palms of her hands together and linking her fingers.

"Friday, it is," he said. "Pick you up at seven."

She looked a bit conflicted and he wondered if she needed more time to prepare for their date. He was about to ask her, when she responded, "Okay, I'll be ready!"

They exchanged phone numbers and she gave him her address before driving away.

He was ecstatic to see mild excitement lighting her eyes and he rushed to his car to let out a shout of praise for his mini victory.

That date led to a few others during that month. The more time he spent with her, the more he liked her. Her ways were gentle and peaceful yet everyone knew she was also all about the business at hand.

She would be the first to calmly tell everyone to 'get it together' or insist that they 'think positively,' her voice taking on the tone of a teacher. She was passionate about living a Godly life and definitely about her ministry to children. She watched over the children like a hen and her chickens and the children loved her in return.

On their seventh date, he took her to dinner at a classy restaurant. As they chatted and laughed, he observed the ease at which they related to each other and his love for her peaked to maximum proportions.

After their dinner, he pulled up on the driveway to his apartment and smiled at her after he turned off the ignition. The look on her face sent him into fits of laughter. It was obvious that she thought he was up to no good. In fact, it looked like she had been waiting for a moment such as this to cut him loose. When he finally pulled himself together, he asked, "Why are you giving me that dirty almost angry look?"

"Blake, I'm not that sort of woman," she told him haughtily. "If you think because you took me on a few dates that qualifies you," she paused, "and why are you smiling?"

He rubbed his jaw and his smile widened. "Because you are giving me a great idea."

She blushed. "I-I'm sorry. You always take me home after our dates, so-"

"So you think, I'm about to make passionate love to you," he interjected, gazing lovingly at her. She was wearing the softest shade of pink that showed off her honey brown complexion and dark brown hair.

Feeling the intensity of his gaze, her heart began to pound and she looked away wondering why he had this effect on her. He could have anyone else but he'd gone above and beyond to win her affection.

"I know you're not that sort of woman, Gabby," he said quietly. "Just to let you know though, that I don't plan to make love to any woman until we are married."

She was pleasantly surprised by that bit of information because she had no intention of sleeping with a man until he put a wedding ring on her finger. She looked him in the eye. "That's just beautiful, Blake. Any woman would be happy to hear that."

His gaze lingered on her lips as she spoke, before moving to her eyes. Her light brown eyes held him captive. They had gone dark and wide and...deeply sensuous. *She can pretend all she wants, but her eyes are saying it all.* "Any woman?" he asked huskily, the air thick with the tension of their awakened desire.

Gabrielle was glad she was sitting down because she could barely think straight. She had no answer for his question. Well, she couldn't lie and, it was inappropriate to declare herself that woman. Her eyes grew wider and her lips parted ever so slightly as she wrestled with how to respond. The truth would be great but she had no intention of admitting her love for any man before he confessed his love for her. So, she continued to gaze into Blake's dark brown eyes, and allow her heart to soar and dream.

Feeling powerless in his emotional state, Blake knew they were on dangerous grounds. He broke their gaze, leaning his head against the headrest, and staring through the windshield. He heard her shallow breathing as she fought to regain control of her feelings and he knew that she wasn't as unaware of the intense attraction between them as he'd thought. Shaking himself out of his thoughts, he brought his eyes back to hers. "I wanted you to hear something," he said quietly, "and that's why I was making a brief stop at my home before taking you home."

Her expression reflected a mixture of relief and anticipation, as she told him softly, "Okay. I'll come in."

A few minutes later, Blake asked her to leave her purse on the sofa and sit in front of his keyboard on a stool in the living room.

She watched curiously as he slid on the seat behind the keyboard. His body language told her not to ask questions.

He looked at her, feeling the familiar blissful jolt in his heart that confirmed he was making the right decision. "This is for you," he told her as he struck the keys on the keyboard.

"Okay!" She smiled at him, listening to the instrumental and thinking the tune sounded familiar.

He began to sing.

"Oh...my...gosh! That's "Hello," she squealed, unable to contain her excitement. "One of my favorites from Lionel Richie!" Then blushing, she covered her face with both hands and began to peep at him through her fingers.

He smiled at her, tickled by her girlish behavior as he sang the last lines of the song. But, when the song ended with, "I love you," he was surprised to see tears in her eyes. He rushed to her side and kneeled on the floor before her, his hands grasping one of hers. "Are you okay?"

"Yes." She gazed affectionately at him. "Thank you. That was beautiful." She caressed his cheek with her hand.

He gazed up at her and knew...he had fallen hard for her. Then, he heard himself say three unforgettable words, "I love you."

"I love you, too," she said softly. "And all that you represent."

His eyes held hers for a moment, warmly and tenderly, before trailing down her body. "You're so beautiful," he said softly.

"So are you," she responded smiling. "Beautifully handsome."

"Can you be in an exclusive relationship with me?" he asked.

"Absolutely," she responded, her eyes dancing with delight. "I would love that."

Elated, he jumped to his feet and pulled her into his arms. "I will always love you," he told her, lowering his head so that his lips were inches from hers. He gazed at her slightly parted full lips. *Mercy! This mouth is giving me all kinds of ideas.*

Her heart racing with love, she wrapped her arms tightly around his waist. Her eyes slid shut, and sentimental thoughts began to swirl in her mind as she eagerly waited for his lips. She waited, and waited, feeling the warmth of his breath on her face. What on earth? Her eyes fluttered open, only to see him in the same holding pattern...waiting.

She looked in his eyes and knew he was waiting for her to be a willing and active participant in their first kiss. She unclasped her hands from his waist to wrap them around his neck and tilted her head towards his lips. He moaned softly as his lips captured the delicate fullness of her mouth. The gentleness of their kiss sent heat and desire coursing through their veins. He was careful not to let his hands wander too far below her shoulders or to kiss her too deeply. And, when she started making soft, inarticulate sounds, he pulled his lips away from hers and cradled her limp body in his arms.

She could feel his heart beating rapidly in his chest, where she buried her face, blatantly breathing in his male scent as she basked in the absolutely delightful moment.

"I believe it's time to go," he told her, breathing deeply above her head.

She swallowed the lump in her throat as he released her and nodded, not trusting her voice.

The fifteen-minute journey to her home was blissfully quiet. When he pulled up at her apartment they were still struggling to quench their desire for each other. That night, they prayed and agreed to limit their physical contact and put their focus on getting to know each other.

Blake took their courtship slowly because Gabrielle always seemed guarded. From their many conversations, he knew she felt short-changed by others. Always restrained, he was pleasantly surprised that on one of their dates, she confessed that she had a rough childhood and that she and her mom did not have a great relationship even to her mother's death. However, she was close to Aunt Jean who now stood in the place of her mother. She had cried on his shoulder that day, and he let her while he prayed for her. Since that day, he had begun praying for her daily because he knew she would have to tear down all the barriers that she'd erected around her heart for them to move forward in their relationship.

Almost eight months later, prostrate before the Lord on the floor in his bedroom, Blake knew he still wanted Gabby in his life...perhaps from the moment he first laid eyes on her. He could not recall ever desiring a woman as much as he desired her...not just to fulfill his fleshly desires but to nurture the longings of his soul.

He was confident that they had the forever kind of love. She was a keeper, a rare gem that he could not live without. They were on the same page and she could easily calm him with the gentleness in her voice. *And, what a great heart!* It was even more amazing that she was not fully aware of the effect she had on him.

One Sunday evening, she fell asleep on the sofa in his apartment. She had visited him ahead of the others on the committee that was planning the church's Christmas theatrical production. He smiled, gazing at her slender yet curvy frame before pulling the brown throw over her shoulders. There was something very serene and beautiful about the way she was curled up, almost in a fetal position, her arms held together loosely at her chest. She was the most beautiful creature he'd ever seen...so exquisite. He kneeled at the sofa, and moved a strand of hair from her forehead. He loved the soft texture of her hair and he loved the way it smelled too.

"I love you," he told her softly, caressing her cheek with his hand.

She stirred and her eyelids fluttered open, then she gently held his hand to her cheek. "I love you, too," she said, smiling.

The way her eyes light up whenever she smiles, makes her even more beautiful. His heart was engulfed with joy and he returned her smile, feeling a sudden urge to nibble on her lips. "Will you marry me?" he asked, staring at her as if he could see deep down into her soul.

Her eyes widened and she sat up on the sofa, a beautiful, healthy glow on her face. She leaned forward and cupped his face with her hands. "Yes! Thought you would never ask," she said gently, planting a tender kiss on his lips.

He swept her up in his arms, burning against her as he kissed her thoroughly.

She wanted him just as much as he wanted her. It was sheer agony to keep their emotions in check. But, reluctantly they did.

Four months later, in spring of the following year, they were married and since then, they had been inseparable…well, so he thought.

Blake exhaled deeply as he came out of his musings. Sleep was nowhere in sight so he rolled on his side as questions floated through his mind.

Where did I fall short in our relationship?
Did I not satisfy her physically or emotionally?
Did I not give her enough attention?
Did I take her love for granted?

Without much effort, vivid memories of the way they were, ravaged his mind, and his body reminded him of a need that was long overdue.

An immense sense of loss struck him.

He'd loved so many things about Gabrielle, her strength, her creative imagination and definitely the way she was not afraid to express her love for him. In fact, he adored her. Maybe he'd even put her on a golden pedestal. One that he'd unconsciously built, for the only person suitable for the category...infallible.

CHAPTER 11

SISTERHOOD

Gabrielle drew back the curtains in the laundry area to catch a glimpse of what promised to be a cool Saturday morning, before pulling clothes from the dryer and placing them in the laundry basket. *Why do I keep forgetting I am doing laundry?* she pondered.

Ever since Blake left, her routines had become somewhat helter-skelter, causing her to be in survival mode. She had started doing the laundry on Friday evenings again, in the hope of getting back into some sort of a routine.

"This is an unwelcomed habit," she scolded herself as she removed half dried clothes from the washer to the dryer, then turning on the dryer. She closed the door to the laundry area locking out the humming sound of the dryer.

Grabbing the handles of the laundry basket, she walked to her room, sat on the bed and began folding the towels. She smiled to herself then broke out in giggles. *He sure couldn't fold towels.* At two different times, she'd asked Blake to fold and stack the towel closet after they had done the laundry. But after inspecting the towel closet the second time around, she'd decided that this was not his thing. The entire closet seemed ransacked. It was pathetic. She grinned even more when she remembered the proud, it's-all-done look on Blake's face.

The ringing of her cell phone brought an end to her reflections and she hastily searched on the bed until she found it.

Unknown number.

She slumped back on the pillows wondering if she should take the call. She decided not to answer it. *What if it's Larry Kanate?*

110

After their incident, she had ignored Larry's calls. But the following week, he had called from a different number begging for her forgiveness. Just thinking about their telephone conversation annoyed her.

"Gabrielle, please don't hang up!" Larry had begged.

She'd almost kicked herself for answering the unknown number. "What do you want?" she asked firmly.

"I know what happened between us was unexpected. Are you okay?" Larry sounded genuinely concerned, but she'd closed her ears and heart to his pitiful, tormented voice.

"Gabrielle?"

"Is that it?" she asked stiffly.

"Please don't tell Rozene," he blurted out.

Her sharp intake of breath caused a pain in her heart and she bolted upright on her bed and told him in no uncertain terms through clenched teeth, "No. I will NOT tell your wife you take advantage of unsuspecting females," before disconnecting the call.

She had had it with Larry Kanate.

Thanks to him, she had taken sick leave from her previous job, then eventually resigned after quickly picking up her current job. Other than their run-in in Talpher Supermarket, she was thankful that she hadn't heard from him for several months.

Gabrielle released a shallow breath as the phone stopped ringing. *That takes care of that*, she thought. But, the phone started ringing again. *A persistent caller.*

"Hello! Happy Saturday!" Gabrielle answered cheerfully.

"Gabrielle, please don't hang up!"

Her insides jolted at the sound of Larry's voice and she clutched the phone in a death grip. *Was he having another epiphany?*

"What do you want," she asked firmly, fighting to keep the annoyance out of her voice.

"I'm so sorry for what I di-did to you." Larry's voice broke. "I just wondered if we could meet and talk."

Gabrielle lifted her eyes to the ceiling. "Larry, you already told me you're sorry. There won't be any meeting."

"I really feel bad about my actions, Gabrielle. I have never done anything like that in my entire life. My Pastor thinks it's a good idea to meet with you, preferably face to face."

"Larry, I told you there will be no meeting. STOP calling my phone or I WILL report you to the police." With that she disconnected the call. She hissed her teeth. "What in the world do we have to talk about?" she said loudly. "That man is trying to make me lose my testimony."

Lying on the bed, she looked up at the ceiling thinking, *The nerve! Isn't it enough you've ruined my marriage? No doubt, you need serious prayers.* Vapors of unhappiness shrouded the atmosphere as memories of the terrible incident with Larry engulfed her mind. *I'm becoming depressed again. Time to fix that.*

Deciding that same moment she needed not stay home all weekend, she thought about seeing a movie later that evening and started to make plans for the coming week. She rolled on her side to pick up the home phone from the nightstand then spread out on her bed again. She dialed Vivian's cell phone number.

Vivian picked up the phone after a few rings. "Hey, hey, Gabby!"

"Hey, hey, my 'sister.' I know you're off on Monday. How about an early dinner?"

"Of course! You know I'm trying to escape from my peeps. How about Alessa? You like their soups and salads," Vivian responded amiably.

"Alessa it is," Gabrielle agreed, then added. "Thanks, Viv! But I know you don't want to be away from that man of God and not to mention your beautiful daughter."

Vivian chuckled knowingly. "Okay. Guilty, I can't live without them. But, I want to spend time with you."

"Awww. Thanks! See you soon."

"Don't forget you'd promised to take Angelica to the park after church tomorrow."

"Yep, we're on. Girls day out."

"All set then. See you tomorrow, James is trying to get my attention."

"Okay. Bye!"

Gabrielle couldn't help but smile as she disconnected the call. Vivian had been a tower of strength and the voice of reason, many times in her life.

It was Vivian who had noticed a change in her appetite and had teased her that she was pregnant during lunch at school.

If only it was a joke.

When she'd missed her period, she and Vivian went to the pharmacy after school and bought a pregnancy test kit. Shell-shock would not aptly describe their faces when the test stick registered positive in the bathroom at Gabrielle's home. Thankfully, her mother was not yet home. Vivian was the first to recover as Gabrielle's eyes grew larger by the second.

"I know you feel like panicking, but don't," Vivian encouraged her. "It's going to be alright."

Gabrielle let out a loud scream before collapsing on the bathroom floor.

She had kept her pregnancy a secret from her mother but when she and Vivian visited the Women's Clinic, and the doctor confirmed that she was over six weeks pregnant, she knew she had to give her mother the unwelcomed news.

That same evening, Vivian's mother gave her the go ahead to sleepover, since they had a test the following day and they usually studied together. They had always been "A" students and they had plans to attend college after high school. However, the truth was that, Vivian also wanted to be with Gabrielle when she broke the news of her pregnancy to her mother.

After dinner at Gabrielle's home, she and Vivian washed then stacked the dishes in the cupboards. Mrs. Lather appeared to be in a great mood, singing as she scrubbed the stove. The girls hovered until she was finished.

"Mom, I-I need-."

"What is it, Gabrielle?" her Mom asked, in a formal tone. "Stop the stuttering. I told you to get your thoughts together before you open your mouth to speak. Plus, I am spending a fortune to get you the best education there is. You should be able to put two sentences together to express your thoughts. Now, what were you saying?"

Tongue-tied, Gabrielle cringed, casting a furtive glance in Vivian's direction.

"Mrs. Lather," Vivian began, "Gabrielle-"

"Vivian," Mrs. Lather cautioned, "please let Gabrielle speak for herself. Gabrielle stop slouching and speak up."

Vivian pursed her lips, encouraging Gabrielle with her eyes.

Gabrielle's watery eyes bounced around the kitchen before settling on her mother. She straightened her shoulders as her mother observed her shrewdly. "Mom," she said in a voice that even she did not recognize. "I-I'm…" Suddenly, she was at a loss for words.

Her mother flashed impatient eyes to the ceiling before looking at Gabrielle again.

After an unbearable pause, Vivian held Gabrielle's hand in support, and Gabrielle found her voice. "Mom, I am pregnant," she said quietly, looking at the floor to make sure she had a place to land safely when her mother hit her. It would have been the first time but she felt that she deserved it for bringing shame to the family.

"Okay," Mrs. Lather said with raised eyebrows. "Is that all?" She looked intently from one to the other, before saying, "I'll be in my room."

"Mom, please!"

"What's done is done, Gabrielle," Mrs. Lather said, walking away from them as Gabrielle burst into tears.

A few minutes later, Vivian led a weeping Gabrielle to her room, and allowed her to spend the entire night curled up on her lap. Gabrielle remembered Vivian offering words of encouragement and praying each time she drifted in and out of consciousness.

It was business as usual for Mrs. Lather in the following weeks. She never mentioned the conversation she had with Gabrielle or inquired about her pregnancy.

Meanwhile, Vivian was busy attempting to convince Gabrielle to let some good come out of the dreadful incident with Jesse by carrying the baby. "God is going to work it out for your good," Vivian told her. "You just wait and see."

During that time, Gabrielle began leaning on Aunt Jean, who lived three houses from her home. She provided constant support to Gabrielle, answering all her questions about motherhood and encouraging her to stay positive, despite her mother's behavior towards her.

One evening, Gabrielle had come home early from school and heard her mother and Aunt Jean arguing. She had quietly slipped into her bedroom and closed the door.

She just knew that Aunt Jean was trying to convince her mother that their lives would still be perfect even with a grandchild.

By week eight, she and Vivian were back at the Women's Clinic looking at the sonogram of the precious life that she was carrying inside her womb. Although she was barely showing, she'd acknowledged for the first time that she was carrying a priceless gift within.

A few days later, as she and Vivian came off the school bus and took their five-minute walk home, Vivian appointed herself God-mother and whipped out a pink teddy bear with a white ribbon around its neck.

"My first of many gifts for my God-child," she declared. "It's a girl. We need to start thinking about names."

Gabrielle shook her head then looked at Vivian quizzically. "You're hoping for a girl?"

"Kill joy!" Vivian eyed her. "We'll find out in a few weeks."

Gabrielle sighed. "At least somebody is totally overjoyed."

"I know we don't have all the answers but we will work it out. I know this is not how you dreamed your life would be, and we'd always said that we would remain virgins until our wedding night. Still, my prayer is that you'll find peace in your heart as you carry this child. I know God is going to give you a husband who will love and cherish you. God will take care of you. You just wait and see."

Gabrielle smiled at her. Such wisdom always flowed from her. She was wise beyond her years. "Thanks, Viv! You are my friend for life."

"Right back at you!"

That Thursday night, Gabrielle kneeled by her bedside and settled in her heart that she was going to carry this child. A few minutes later, she whipped out several sheets of pink letter size paper and decided to start writing letters daily to her unborn child. Her joy increased as she expressed her emotions on paper. But, that joy was short-lived. The following Saturday morning, she woke up and she was spotting. By the time paramedics arrived, she had suffered a miscarriage.

CHAPTER 12

UNDESIRABLE SITUATION

Now the devastation was over, Blake told Bishop Clandon that his faith was stronger and he was now ready to continue his duties as worship leader. But Bishop Clandon had instead asked him, 'if he was ready to resume his duties at home.' Caught by surprise, Blake did not know how to respond so he kept silent.

Bishop Clandon eyed him from across his desk in the church office. "Have you ever thought about the underlying reason why Gabrielle would do what she did? You and I know that kind of behavior is outside of her character. For what it is worth, you should see her and have that conversation with her."

Blake stuttered, "I-I…" Realization dawned in his eyes as he remembered Quincy saying the same thing.

"I know you didn't think about that," Bishop Clandon filled in. "Life has a way of catching up with us when we don't deal with past issues. Just maybe there is something she kept from you. And, you may also want to tell her how you feel about her infidelity. It would be good for both of you."

Blake stared blindly. "Talk? I don't know if I want to do that, Bishop."

"It wouldn't hurt to find out, Son." Bishop Clandon smiled. "Pray about it and give it some thought."

Blake nodded and then said goodbye.

A few minutes later, he sat in his car in the parking lot at church thinking about Bishop Clandon's suggestion. His heart longed for Gabrielle but he just didn't know if he could or was willing to 'resume his duties at home.' Truth be told, he missed her…missed her badly. That much he was willing to admit to himself, although things had gotten a lot better with him.

A hint of a smile curled up at the corners of his lips as sweet memories of Gabrielle filled his mind. Strangely, he did not resist. She had been his love match, his resting place, his everything. His smile widened into a grin when he remembered her "double dare" expression, whenever she would encourage him to follow her latest pursuit. Like the time when she decided that doing Pilates would be her next big thing.

She had purchased a beginner's Pilates video and invited him to participate in the family fitness room one Saturday morning. Lying on his side on the exercise mat, he watched the rays of the early morning sunlight slanting through the windows, bathing her in its light. Her pony tail swayed back and forth, her body flexible as it yielded to the demands of the Pilates.

It was hard to take his eyes off her. Every move she made caused him to feel more alive. His whole body aflame, he knew it was his time to issue a "double dare." He made a low guttural sound and she glanced at him.

"You're not moving," she said, giving him one of her get-it-together looks. "You promised to…" she paused, and he could tell her senses were reeling as she gazed into the smoldering fire in his eyes.

He flashed her one of his irresistible smiles and she giggled before pulling herself together to waggle a finger at him.

That was all the encouragement he needed, a quick roll and he was by her side. He pulled her forward onto his chest, and pressed his hot lips to hers in a fierce, demanding kiss, smothering the protest that was springing from her delectable lips. She let out a soft cry, whimpering in pleasure then clutched his cheeks with both hands and surrendered to the moment.

Overpowering warmth engulfed Blake at the memory and he gripped the steering wheel. His facial muscles tensed and he shifted in his seat, reprimanding himself for his lapse in judgment. The sensations he felt were not new, just unwanted…a definite waste of his time. Yet, the challenge was to keep them at bay.

Pulling out of the parking lot, he continued to mull over Bishop Clandon's request. *Was this a divine setup?*

He was still deep in thoughts fifteen minutes later when he pulled up in a parking spot at Zoe's apartment complex. Grabbing his toolkit, he walked to the last door on the first block and rang the doorbell.

Zoe could hardly breathe as she took in Blake's six feet three inches athletic body through the peep hole. He had removed the tie he wore to church, but was still wearing a gray fitted jacket, a pair of gray pants and a red shirt that was opened at the top to reveal a hint of hair on his chest. She licked her lips as she gazed at his broad muscular shoulders, flat abs and well-proportioned body. *That man should not be so fine! Certainly not a waste of God's clay*, she thought.

Almost breathless, she pulled the door open and gave Blake her sunniest smile. "Welcome to my humble abode," she hugged him, pressing her body against him in an attempt to bask in the healthy glow of his caramel colored skin.

"Hey, friend." Blake greeted her, taken by the warm reception he was receiving, but quickly pulling out of her embrace.

Her gaze slid over him before closing the door. *He feels as fine as he looks. He can deny it all he wants but the feeling he is evoking in me has nothing to do with friendship.* "You smell great," she told him teasingly.

"Thanks!" Blake smiled at her, taking in her coffee colored skin that highlighted her dark brown almond shaped eyes. Her glossy brown hair fell over her shoulders in tiny, barrel-like curls. "Where are the boys?"

"They went to the park with their grandmother." Her eyes twinkled. "They'll be back later," she added softly. *We are alone*, she wanted to add.

"Okay. Where is your new computer?"

"In the study. Would you like something to drink before you start?" she asked leading the way.

"No. I am good. Let's get you all squared away."

She touched his arm playfully as they came to a stop in the living room. "You are all about the work, huh?"

He couldn't help but smile at her. "Business before pleasure. Let's go."

Blake followed Zoe as she sashayed across the tiled floor in the living room, then down a narrow hallway. Clearly, she'd taken some time to perfect that walk. An air of seduction marked her movements and the soft fabric of her long backless red dress clung to her stunning, voluptuous figure. *Is it my imagination or is Zoe flirting with me?* Notwithstanding, Zoe Thurman was a strikingly beautiful woman, he concluded.

Zoe entered the study and pointed at her new computer in the corner next to the desk. Blake walked over to retrieve it and Zoe watched him as he pulled it away from the desk and opened the box. He exuded strength and confidence every step of the way. Unable to help herself, she reached down and squeezed his arm. "Do you need me to do anything?" she asked, smiling and cozying up to him. "I want to help."

"Okay, Miss Handy-Lady, please hand me my tools when I ask for them." He grinned at her. "You better know what is what."

She winked at him. "You know I got you covered."

"You better," he told her. "Is this the desk that is wobbly?"

"Yes. A few of the screws fell out. Let me get them," Zoe said, pulling out a drawer and scooping up the screws. She handed them to Blake.

"Okay. I will take care of the table first."

Forty-five minutes later, Zoe clapped enthusiastically as she inspected the applications and features on her new Apple desktop that was now sitting on the desk that Blake had repaired. "Amazing! Thanks so much, Blake," she hugged him then kissed his cheek.

"You're welcome," Blake responded, moving out of her embrace. He closed the clasp on his toolkit and moved to the door signaling he was ready to leave.

Zoe tossed her hair behind her shoulders and smiled teasingly at him before sauntering ahead of him in silence, back to the living room.

"You must be thirsty by now." Her gaze fixed on Blake, awaiting his response.

"I'm good."

She feigned disgruntlement, pouting her lips. "You really don't want anything, not even water."

A smile spread across his face. "Water, please."

"Okay, finally!" She clapped her hands. "Have a seat and let me get it for you."

Blake took a seat on the huge black leather sofa. His eyes circled the living room, taking in the splash of red accent in the decor, matching Zoe's vibrant personality. He did not know much about her except on a church level. However, he knew that she wasn't married. Several of the men at church had confessed to him that they had crushes on her and her shapely hourglass figure, which Zoe was not afraid to show off or use to her advantage. He'd observed that she was a bold, confident woman who knew what she wanted and was not afraid to reach for it.

Zoe returned with two bottles of water. She leaned forward as she gave Blake one, giving him a full view of her ample cleavage.

He stared into her eyes, not flinching. *What man in his right mind wouldn't take advantage of this opportunity?* An inner voice cautioned him, *Don't forget who you are.* He broke eye contact with her and took the water from her hand. "Thanks," he said, twisting the cap from the bottle and began drinking.

Zoe couldn't help but wonder what he was thinking as she sat beside him on the sofa. He seemed so impenetrable. She wished he would give her something to hold on to…a little hint that he was interested. She had to find a way to soften him up, to reach his beautiful heart.

"So, how much do I owe for the pleasure of your company?" she purred, gazing at him with hooded eyes for a couple of seconds before leaning forward. "I am willing to pay in cash or kind," she laughed coyly, her eyes showing her full appreciation of his anatomy.

Blake didn't say anything for a few minutes. "No payment necessary." He looked at her. "Zoe, you do know I'm married, right?"

She held his gaze. "And?"

"While I enjoy your company, I don't play like that."

She leaned back with arched brows. "Why did you come here, Blake? You knew what I wanted."

"You asked me to help you set up your new computer and to repair your desk. That's why, I'm here."

She gave a hollow laugh. "That's not what your body is communicating to me."

Blake took a moment and seemed to choose his next words carefully. He doubted any man had ever said no to her. "In the grand scheme of things, it really doesn't matter what my body wants. My body is subject to the will of the

Lord. I have already committed myself to my wife so my body belongs to her."

"Really?" she scoffed. "From what I've been hearing, ain't nothing going on between you two."

Blake got up abruptly, grabbed his toolkit and marched towards the front door. "I will see myself out. Have a good-"

"I did offer to pay in kind," Zoe interjected.

"Stop saying-" Blake turned to face her and almost swallowed his tongue. Zoe was standing and exposing all that God gave her. He stood transfixed as she moved towards him and came to a standstill inches from him. She tossed her hair over her shoulders.

"Tell me, you don't like what you see," she dared him, arching her chest.

Heat flushed Blake's body as his eyes took a noticeable trek over her body, and then latched onto her supple breasts.

"All yours," she encouraged smiling, extending them in offering, "you need me and I definitely need you."

Perturbed, Blake shook his head, as the popular saying, *"where freeness exists, it's folly to resist,'* flushed his brain. He looked into Zoe's eyes, and it took every muscle in his body to turn away from her.

"I have to go," he said breathlessly. And without waiting for her response, he literally ran to the door, swung it open, and dashed to his car. Switching on the ignition, he quickly reversed and drove out of the apartment complex.

"Thank you, Jesus. Thank you, Jesus," was all he kept muttering, all the way home.

CHAPTER 13

COURAGE TO BELIEVE

"Aren't you looking like the rays of the evening sunshine," Vivian greeted Gabrielle with a hug before taking her place across the table from her at Alessa Italian Restaurant. Gabrielle was decked out in a cream-colored sweater, a pair of brown jeans, and brown mid-calf length boots.

Gabrielle chuckled. "Look who's talking, Miss Everyday-Is-A-Great-Day!"

With her blunt cut hair style, medium frame and large, dark brown eyes, Vivian looked great in a long sleeve red fitted shirt, a pair of black jeans, and black knee high boots.

"Awww! You are in a great mood. So happy to see that," Vivian remarked smiling.

"Right back at you!" Gabrielle responded, returning her smile. "I took the liberty of ordering for you. Got our favorite spot too, front and corner booth."

Vivian laughed giving her an eyebrow lift as the waiter placed their soups before them. "And folks, that's what happens when you know your 'sister.'"

"Oh, yes," Gabrielle agreed smiling.

Vivian prayed and they dived in to their soups.

"Vegetable soup?" Vivian grimaced.

Gabrielle eyed her. "Don't look like that. It's Cheese-Topped Vegetable soup. I know you're watching your calorie intake, and mine."

Vivian playfully knitted her brows. "You know I have to watch your calorie intake."

"Yes. Please do because I have no time to read labels anymore," Gabrielle grinned at her. "Can't be seen standing around in any supermarket. Larry might sneak up on me."

Vivian laughed out loud. "I know it's not funny but I still grin every time I think about what happened with you and Larry in Talpher Supermarket." She shook her head. "You made Larry chase you out of Talpher."

"Yep. It was not my proudest or my bravest moment, but I live to fight again."

"Yes, you do."

"And speaking of Larry, he called again," Gabrielle mentioned, taking in a spoonful of Cream of Tomato soup.

Vivian lifted her eyes to the ceiling. "What does he want? Is he bothering you? Do we need to get a restraining order?"

Gabrielle sighed. "No." She then recounted her conversation with Larry.

"No, he didn't." Vivian was clearly disgusted. "That man makes me have violent thoughts. His poor wife."

"Rozene is strong," Gabrielle told her. "She knows how to handle Larry."

"I hope so," Vivian said.

"Something bothered me about…the incident with Larry," Gabrielle said, staring at her soup. "Viv, I just stood there, hoping for it to be over quickly. I just stood there. Frozen. Barely fighting. Ugh! Worst. I kept silent after the incident, as I did with Jesse. Now, I am looking back and I can see why I kept silent. It was fear. But, thank you, Jesus, no more. I have regained my voice and I will not be silent."

Vivian touched Gabrielle's hand across the table. "You are a fighter, Gabby, and you know it. But sometimes when we don't deal with past issues they become giants in our lives. But, I'm so glad you've gotten past that."

"For sure!" Gabrielle confirmed. "I always knew that when I am frustrated and tired, I will do irrational things but what happened with Larry is sure proof."

Frowning, Vivian held up her hand. "You indicated you wanted him to stop several times, if I remember correctly."

"Aside from that, I should never have put myself in that position, Viv. A massage from my boss? Good Lord! That kind of behavior is not me, in no way, shape or form."

"Yes. It's not like you to do something like that," Vivian agreed. "But, I think Larry had a secret crush on you." She eyed Gabrielle as she began to protest. "Let me finish. And, perhaps you didn't realize."

"I caught him staring a few times but didn't think anything of it. Honestly, Viv, Larry didn't strike me as the kind of man to force himself on a woman."

"Something must be going on with him. He may be hiding a very dark past."

Gabrielle paused, studying her soup for a moment, before looking up. "You know what? Let's add Larry and Rozene to our prayer list."

It was Vivian's turn to pause. She looked at Gabrielle with tears brimming. "You my dear 'sister' just testified to the awesome work that God has been doing in your life." She then reached across the table and placed her hand on Gabrielle's. "Thank you for that. You have always had a great heart, Gabby. Please do not lose that beautiful part of you. "

Gabrielle clutched her friend's hand before letting go. "It is the working of the Lord. But, I must confess I did kick my bedpost when I thought about Larry's call. In fact, I will kick him on his shin when I see him next time. I'm going all out ninja on him."

"Right! Don't forget I've known you for umpteen years. My only regret is that I wasn't here initially to help you through all of this."

"Not mad at you. I know you had to go on your family vacation." Suddenly, Gabrielle was all choked up. "Thanks for all you did to bring me back to life. The support that came from you and the other members of our prayer circle has been tremendous."

Vivian smiled. "The pleasure was ours. So glad to see you're in a great place."

Gabrielle returned her smile. "God is good. There were days when… I didn't think I would make it."

"God's good," Vivian agreed.

Gabrielle cleared her throat and then took in a spoonful of her soup, before saying, "If anybody had told me that I would have been a victim of rape, I would probably tell them to stop lying." A slight smile played on Gabrielle's lips. *Did I just say rape? I have come a long way,* she thought.

Vivian looked her in the eye. "I am so glad you survived that. What the enemy plans for evil, God will turn it in your favor."

"Amen to that," Gabrielle agreed.

"Have you been browsing the Sunday School training material?" Vivian asked. "Hopefully, you'll return soon."

"Yes. I'm still going through the material. Looking forward to returning, it's been a while."

Vivian smiled. "Yes. I miss you but I know the kids miss you more. They have been inquiring but I told them you are on a sabbatical. One smarty pants dared to tell me, 'Sister Montgomery is not on sabbatical. I've been seeing her at church.'"

Gabrielle laughed out. "That sounds just like Ross."

"You got that right," Vivian grinned. "That Ross! Never a dull moment with him around."

"Never," Gabrielle said, briefly shaking her head from side to side. "How is my lovely goddaughter doing? Can't wait for her party, huh?"

Vivian pursed her lips together tightly in a straight line before responding. "She's doing great. But, as usual, she's trying to be the boss of me. She cannot wait to be ten years old. In her mind, something awesome will take place in her life."

Motherhood had been great but definitely a huge learning experience. Both she and James had wanted a child, right after they got married. So they decided to go for it. Only, it took three years before the arrival of Angelica. They had been trying since then for a second child.

Gabrielle grinned at her. "Sounds like Angelica to me."

"Definitely!" A soft chuckle escaped Vivian's lips and her eyes lit with amusement. "Thanks for helping with preparations for her party. She already made her guest list. Of course you and Blake are at the top of the adult column. I know it will be a little strange for both of you to be in close proximity but I will do everything in my power to ensure that you are comfortable."

"It's okay. I'll be alright," Gabrielle smiled slightly, putting Vivian at ease. "We should be at the top of the guest list, we're her favorite aunt and uncle."

Vivian grinned at her. "Can't deny that one. Thanks for taking her to the park."

Gabrielle waved her away. "You are welcome! I'm looking forward to treating Angelica for her birthday."

"Thanks! That will be a great gift for her. She's looking forward to getting dolled up at the hair dresser and doing a mani and pedi. You and Blake seem to always come up with birthday stuff that she loves."

"We try!" she said nonchalantly, causing Vivian to giggle.

"You sure 'hit the nail on the head.'"

"How excited are you for James?" Gabrielle asked. "His ordination ceremony is coming up. Bishop Clandon relies on him so much. It's just right that he'll be ordained. Plus, he is such a great teacher of the Word."

"Sooo excited for my honey. He's a little nervous about all that comes with being a Deacon. I had to remind him of one of my favorite scriptures, ""I will instruct you and teach you in the way you should go; I will guide you with My eye.""

"That's beautiful." Gabrielle smiled and then became quiet.

Vivian looked at her, feeling that she had something important to say.

Finally, Gabrielle said, "I'm thinking of doing away with my 'comfort' box."

Vivian ate some of her soup before looking at Gabrielle. "You're ready, huh?"

"Yes, I think it's time." She gave Vivian a wry smile. "You should be happy. You always thought I should have gotten rid of it a long time ago, but definitely before I got married."

"You took your own time to make that decision and I am proud of you. That box has been with us ever since-"

"Exactly why I need to just leave those memories behind," Gabrielle interjected.

Tears blinded Vivian's eyes. "Well, let me know if I can help in any way with the disposal. I am very proud of your decision."

Gabrielle gave her a tight smile. It was not easy to come to that decision but it was one that she knew she had to make. "I will let you know. And stop "tearing up" before I start doing the same. I need to dispose of my 'comfort' box if I am going to successfully navigate the next leg of my journey."

"Okay. I have it together," Vivian promised, drying her eyes with a napkin from the table. "And speaking of journey, are you making any progress with Blake?"

Gabrielle nibbled on her lips for a moment. "No. Not really."

Vivian studied her for a moment. "What's stopping you from telling Blake the truth about your childhood and letting him take it from there?"

Gabrielle's eyes widened in dismay and the tiny hairs on the back of her neck lifted in alarm. "Tell, Blake?" Momentarily an emotional battle took place within her. She looked at Vivian hesitantly and then bit her lips nervously. "I just, just can't."

"Why not?" Vivian asked, pressing her.

Agonizing, Gabrielle confessed. "His eyes were once filled with love for me and I can't bear to see the pain, judgment, and scorn they now hold. I always remembered how he would gaze at me with adoration before we actually started dating, trying to gain my affection. Even though I spurned him, he wouldn't give up. I just wasn't used to anyone wanting to give me affection so badly, didn't think I deserved it." She gave a slight chuckle. "I couldn't even understand my own reaction to him, just being in his presence made me want to talk gibberish. And after we got married, he would look at me as if I took his breath away." She paused. *What I would do for him to look at me like that again.* "I can't, Viv. Another rejection from him would send me over the edge. I am not strong enough to withstand that."

Determination darkened Vivian's gaze. "That is a lie from the enemy to keep you bound. He is killing your expectations and any desire you have to regain Blake's trust and love. You looove Blake. I remember when you both decided to date exclusively," she paused beaming, "oh, the joy and radiance from a love waited for and given in the right season. You exuded happiness in every movement."

Gabrielle couldn't help but smile. "Great times."

"Yes. And after you got married, my word, Girl - you looked like love. You told me that you didn't even know you had that place in your heart that only a special type of love could find and fill. I believe those beautiful times are worth fighting for."

"I know but I'm afraid. Plus, I see Zoe Thurman hanging on to his every word at church. And, he's enjoying her company."

"What? Girl, stop! You know your husband is not that kind of man."

"That's what I thought about Larry and look what happened."

"Don't you dare compare Blake with Larry," Vivian hissed. "I don't know Larry but Blake is a good man. This is just a setback. Trust God, trust His timing, and let Him guide you."

Gabrielle stared blindly at the wall beyond Vivian before hanging her head. Her internal struggles were evident.

"God has equipped you to overcome all the challenges that life throws at you," Vivian encouraged. "Draw on the power of the Lord Jesus Christ that's in you. "Greater is He that is in you than he that is in the world.""

Gabrielle nodded and slowly pursed her lips.

"Gabby," Vivian encouraged, "don't die in a place that was only meant for you to pass through. Be brave. Ask God for the hard thing. Tell Him you need your husband back at home where he belongs. Tell Him that you are afraid, frightened to make this request because you feel you don't deserve a second chance. Tell Him that you cannot deal with Blake's rejection. Be real. Tell God everything."

Tears rolled down Gabrielle's cheek as Vivian words hit home and saturated her being. Vivian had put into words all that she wanted to tell the Lord but was ashamed to do so. She gazed blindly at Vivian through her tears. "I needed to hear that," she said, using the napkin to mop her eyes.

"You are just passing through," Vivian stated with a smile.

"I am just passing through," Gabrielle confirmed, returning her smile.

*****

Two hours later, Gabrielle lit scented candles and took a long soak in her favorite baby powder scented bubble bath in her oversized Jacuzzi. Her thoughts centered on her conversation with Vivian. *What's stopping me from telling Blake the truth about my childhood? Well, let me see - There is that little thing called a conversation, which I sense he's not willing to have with me on any such level. Then, there is that look in his eyes - anger, scorn, judgment - that burns my heart, every time. And, let me not forget, the discomfort and embarrassment I feel every time I see him.*

Too many thoughts were circulating through her mind. She closed her eyes and exhaled deeply, attempting to cope with the current state of her frail nerves. The water felt cool and refreshing on her body, relaxing her. It was just what she needed to shift her energy at the moment.

A few minutes later, she rose from the Jacuzzi then sat on its porcelain edge and gently patted herself dry with a fluffy white towel. She could smell a faint trace of baby powder on her skin as she applied generous amounts of body lotion before slipping into her sleep shirt.

133

Unconsciously engrossed in the longings of her heart, she was placing the lotion in a basket on the ground near the Jacuzzi when a long sigh escaped her lips. *If I could just turn back time.*

She walked silently to the sink, turned on the faucet and bent down to splash cool water on her face. After turning off the faucet, she dried her face with a small towel that was hanging on the towel rack near the sink. Her eyes traveled her face in the lighted mirror above the sink. Pain and a hint of fear displayed in her eyes.

In many ways, so much had changed since her separation from Blake. Now she was longing for the times before the darkness and agony of yesterday. *Lord, I don't want to be like this,* she thought, gripping the sink. *This sad person! I want to be at peace, Lord. I want to live again.*

In her bedroom, she perched upon the pillows on her bed to further commune with God. Vivian's words - 'Don't die in a place that was only meant for you to pass through. Be brave. Ask God for the hard thing'- echoed in her ears.

Inwardly, she felt small. A shadow of her former self.

Having pulled on all her strength to survive, she knew she needed to stop punishing herself and allow herself to heal. She'd learned during the journey that her failure to obey God's word, had caused a horrible shift in her life...and Blake's. She leaned deeper against the pillows, and cried out to God, "*I have sinned Lord and against thee only have I sinned. Turn me to you and I will teach transgressors your ways.*"

Tears streaming down her face, she felt the urge to read Ezekiel 37, so she wiped her eyes with the back of her hands, then reached for her Bible on the nightstand, and flipped there, "*The Valley of dry Bones.*" She read the first eleven verses before pondering on verse 3, "*...Son of man,* *can these bones live? So I answered, O Lord God, You knowest."*

Deep within her heart she felt the Lord was asking her, *"Will your marriage survive?"* and her response, *"O Lord God, thou knowest."* Suddenly, she felt the urgent need to follow the scripture she just read and prophesy over her situation. She kneeled beside her bed and in a loud voice, she shattered the airwaves, praying and declaring the promises of God over herself, then Blake, and next their marriage.

> *"Lord, I come to You knowing I am highly favored and blessed. Lord, keep me on the path of righteousness. Give me discernment to make decisions based on Your revelation so that I will make godly choices.*
>
> *Lord, I declare that I am a person of integrity. Enable me to stand for godly principles and not waver under pressure from others. Father, I know I am created for a higher purpose so help me to walk worthy of the calling on my life.*
>
> *Thank you for my husband, Blake Paul Montgomery - the man of God who you have placed in my life. Thank you, Lord, for giving him a heart that constantly thirsts for your presence. I pray that You will continue to open doors of opportunity for him. Prosper the works of his hands, Lord, to bring him success and fulfillment.*
>
> *Lord, the scripture declares, "He who finds a wife finds a good thing, and obtains favor*

from the Lord." I declare that I am STILL that "good thing," even though I committed sexual infidelity. Lord, I know You have forgiven me. Thank you for Your forgiveness.

Father, I am ready for Blake to come back home but I feel sooooooo undeserving of that privilege. I give that feeling to you. Give me a new heart that will allow me to rise above who I am at this moment. Transform me into the wife you have called me to be.

In the name of Jesus, I reverse every negative word that was spoken over our marriage. I declare that You have blessed our marriage beyond measure. And that together, Blake and I will accomplish great exploits. Lord, I ask that You continue to direct our steps. In the name of Jesus Christ, I pray, Amen."

In the wee hours of the morning, Gabrielle rose from her knees with Isaiah 43:19 engraved in her spirit - *"Behold, I will do a new thing, now it shall spring forth; Shall you not know it? I will even make a road in the wilderness and rivers in the desert."* She then began to give God thanks for the victory for she knew that her work was completed.

CHAPTER 14

FLUTTERING HEARTS

"I'm feeling incredibly excited," Vivian whispered, clutching Gabrielle's arm. "It's like her wedding day."

"I am excited too." Gabrielle smiled at her. "Can't imagine what will happen on her wedding day. Go on, Mother of the Bride, do your thing."

Vivian grinned at her. "As if anyone could stop me."

"The floor is all yours," Gabrielle said, shaking head and smiling as Vivian moved away.

"Are you ready?" Vivian yelled to the crowd of children and few adults.

"Yes!" Everyone shouted, happily.

Yes, indeed! Gabrielle thought. They were ready for the appearance of Angelica to get her birthday party started. It was indeed a Barbie Princess theme party. Shades of pink and white in various patterns detailed everything - the decorations, multi-tiered cake, cupcakes, lollipops, plates, cups, napkins, forks, straws, and gifts.

Vivian grinned back at the crowd of approximately thirty. They were bustling with excitement. "Princess Angelica is eager to meet you. You, who have so graciously decided to join her for this grand birthday celebration."

Squeals of happiness and shouts of joy were sent her way.

"Can't wait to see the princess!"

"Happy to be here!"

"Bring her out!"

"Ready!"

Vivian beamed with pride. "Girls and boys, ladies and gentlemen, I present Princess Angelica, escorted by her father, Sir James Moore." She motioned with her hand for the music to start and everyone waited for the appearance of the 'princess' in the royally decorated living room at the Moore's two-story single family home.

The music started and the crowd cheered as Angelica appeared on the arm of her father, in a hot pink chiffon gown, looking like a Barbie Princess.

Standing around six feet, James' tall, lean frame was wrapped in an impeccably tailored, one-button shawl collar black tuxedo. Pride lit his face as he watched Angelica bow gracefully to the crowd after hugging him. She then took her assigned seat at the top of the semi-circle.

James prayed for Angelica and those in attendance then Vivian cued everyone to start singing the 'happy birthday' song. Soon, it was meal time. The children squealed delightedly as they sampled all the goodies.

"Can't believe, she's all of ten already," Vivian sighed, smiling joyfully in Angelica's direction.

"Yes," Gabrielle agreed, watching as Angelica handed out party favors. "She's growing up fast. Enjoy every moment."

Vivian nodded, eyes brimming with tears. "I'm so thankful to God for her."

"Me too. Happy for you and James," Gabrielle responded squeezing her hand.

Vivian smiled pleasantly at her. "Time to take this party outside. Can you please help Angelica get dressed? Her Barbie short set is laid out on her bed."

"Sure."

Vivian told Angelica to accompany Gabrielle before saying, "We have a treasure hunt and more games and food outside. Please form a line and we will lead you outside." She motioned with her hand for help from the other adults in the room and they moved speedily to get the children in order.

"Princess Angelica will join you shortly," Vivian hollered as Angelica walked elegantly towards Gabrielle. Gabrielle smiled at Angelica thinking, *she's going to be something for the world to behold.*

Upstairs, Angelica quickly donned her cute pink Barbie short set and was ready to rejoin the party.

"You look very nice!" Gabrielle told her.

Angelica hugged her. "Thanks, Aunt Gabrielle."

"You are welcome! Let's not keep your guests waiting."

"Yes, Ma'am!"

Angelica led the way downstairs, then headed down the passage way towards the door leading to the back patio. Suddenly, the door flew open, and Vivian rushed in. She nodded at Gabrielle, her eyes indicating that something was brewing.

Gabrielle understood the signal and waited.

"Sweety," Vivian said to Angelica, "wait by the door for a moment. I need to speak with Aunt Gabrielle."

Angelica walked not too patiently to the door.

Vivian pulled Gabrielle by the hand up the passage way. "Blake is here," she said quietly. "Just stick to the plan. James is chatting with him outside."

Gabrielle was motionless. Running away was definitely beckoning. Even though she knew Blake would be at the party, now that he was actually here, fear crept in her heart. The last thing she wanted was more chatter about her already broken marriage.

"It's going to be okay." Vivian smiled at her. "Just stick to the plan."

"Yes," Gabrielle said, trying to drum up a smile as she spotted Angelica watching them animatedly at the door.

Vivian eyed Gabrielle with concern.

"I'll be alright," Gabrielle declared. Her heart warmed amidst pangs of trepidation as she looked at

139

Vivian. And, once again she was glad she had someone in her corner.

"Ready?" Vivian asked quietly.

"Ready," Gabrielle responded, steeling herself.

They both moved towards Angelica, who looked totally relieved that they were ready at last.

Vivian opened the door to expose the well-manicured lawn and beautifully maintained shrubs in the backyard.

Angelica burst through the door to greet her guests, then squealed loudly, "Uncle Blake!" In a mad dash, she raced towards Blake.

Blake extracted himself from his conversation with James and scooped her up in his arms, twirling around with her.

"My Earth Angel," he exclaimed exuberantly.

Gabrielle watched them, and her heart leaped at the sound of Blake's joyful laughter. He looked so happy, genuinely happy. Perhaps, the happiest she'd seen him in a long while. He would have made an amazing father. Tears threatened and she looked away.

"Uncle Blake," Angelica grinned up at him after he set her back on the ground. "I'm soooo glad to see you." She lifted an eyebrow. "You look the same."

Blake cocked a brow, "I hope so," which sent her into girlish giggles.

"Uncle Blake, you are so funny!"

He smiled at her. "So how's the party going?"

"Just wonderful!" she beamed.

"Great! I have a special gift for you. I hope you like it."

"Yessssss!" Angelica shrieked happily. "Thank you, Uncle Blake. I just know I'm going to love it." She hugged him. "We're about to do the treasure hunt if you want to join us." She looked towards Gabrielle as she walked with

Vivian towards them. "Aunt Gabrielle is overseeing my team. You can join our team if you like."

Blake did not look up, instead he smiled at Angelica. "I believe I'm going to sit this one out."

"It's going to be fun," Angelica motivated him. "Don't miss out!"

"Okay. I will think about it," he said as Angelica left his side.

Gabrielle grimaced. It wasn't her imagination; all eyes were on Blake and Angelica, some darting back to her. She clutched Vivian's hand for support.

"Go ahead. Let's greet him as planned," Vivian hissed. "He'll return the favor."

"What if he spurns me?"

"He won't. Not in public."

With that Vivian almost yanked Gabrielle towards Blake. "You greet him first," Vivian said through clenched teeth. "And for God sake, relax your face. You're not going to the gallows."

Gabrielle couldn't help but grin at her friend. "You're wrong for saying that!"

"Much better." Vivian laughed softly as they arrived before Blake.

Gabrielle felt almost breathless, taking in his strong jaw and sensuous lips as he greeted them with a slight smile. "Hello, ladies!"

Knowing that Gabrielle would not respond, Vivian returned his smile, hoping to give her time to formulate her response. "Blake!" She hugged him. "Great to see you! I see Angelica is more than happy you are here."

Blake chuckled. "Yes. I received a royal welcome. She is something."

"Isn't she?" Vivian shook her head. "Let me get this treasure hunt started," she said moving away and pulling James by the hand. She hoped that Gabrielle would say a quick greeting to Blake then follow her but glancing behind her, she saw both Blake and Gabrielle looking at each other.

Blake patiently watched Gabrielle taking in the entire length of his body, as if committing him to memory. And for reasons unknown to him, his heart warmed at the thought that she was still attracted to him. Yet the absence of her usual happy-to-see-you smile nagged at him. Catching himself, he silently berated himself for the route his imagination had taken.

He looked even better at close range, Gabrielle thought. He was handsomely clad in a royal blue polo shirt and black jeans that hugged his muscular thighs. When she finally coaxed her eyes to his face, his slightly raised eyebrows asked if she was finished with her body scan.

Warmth flushed her entire body. Then sensing that her eyes were still glowing with blissful appreciation of his anatomy, she shifted her gaze over his shoulder, mumbling, "Good to see you."

Fully aware that all eyes were on them, he had no desire to embarrass her. "Hey," he said softly, pulling her gently by the arm.

She did not expect such a move and before she could come to terms with what was happening, she landed on his chest. She clutched his chest to balance herself, frightened by his nearness yet enjoying the sure touch of his hand round her waist.

I'm holding her close, way too close, he thought. Then, contrary to the wishes of the voice in his head, he relished the warmth of her body against his. *What fragrance is that?* The scent of her perfume rose from her neck. And, he liked the smell of it. *Soft and floral.*

His body began to hum with desire and he swallowed hard, unwilling to give in to his fleshly cravings. But when he released her from their embrace, she began to fidget in a bid to release her bracelet which was caught in a piece of thread from one of the buttons on his shirt.

"Sorry," she murmured. "My bracelet-" Her eyes met his, their faces inches apart, and every coherent thought flew from her mind. Butterflies ran around wildly in her stomach, and her breath hitched as she tried to regain her composure. She blushed, dropping her eyes to his lips, and had to grit her teeth to prevent herself from kissing him. She glanced at him again and from the slow smile that was curling his lips, she knew he had read her mind. *Awkward! Must get away!* "Help me release-"

"Hold still," he said, before breaking the thread between the button and her bracelet.

She fiddled with her bracelet then gave him a grateful look. "Thanks." She realized he'd only hugged her to save her from the wagging tongues.

Before he could respond, she heard Vivian screaming for her. She turned and saw Vivian waving. "We are ready for the treasure hunt," Vivian yelled.

Gabrielle cast a hasty glance at Blake and she saw a touch of something in his eyes – compassion, maybe.

"Go ahead," he told her quietly and she promptly left his side, breathing a little easier. *That was not so bad*, she thought.

Vivian divided the children into two teams for the treasure hunt. Although each team had a captain, Gabrielle and Vivian were the overseers of the teams and Vivian assigned the adults to a team, even though they could not participate. Feeling the need to save Gabrielle, Vivian assigned Blake to her team.

Not that Gabrielle minded.

In fact, not even a tiny bit. She didn't want to deal with Blake in such close proximity. Now, her only job was to ignore the fluttering of her heart each time their eyes connected...which in her estimation was happening way too many times.

She couldn't decide if he was constantly gazing at her or if she was continuously seeking him out during the treasure hunt. Even now they were gazing at each other, a smile touching his lips. Her heart lurched for what seemed an endless moment. *Was his smile a figment of my imagination?* Unable to process what was happening, she smiled back, not wanting to miss the moment. Then unexpectedly, the warm glimmer in his eyes disappeared, replaced by a solemn expression. Her heart sank and she looked beyond him, deciding in that instant to focus her attention on the game. Even so, she kept a watch on him out of her peripheral vision.

What is wrong with you? Blake asked himself as he shifted his gazed from Gabrielle's. Every nerve in his body was attuned to her. There was a gracefulness in her walk and her radiant smile repeatedly jolted his insides. And, as if he needed more encouragement to stare at her, she was checking him out...every second, with those beautiful, expressive eyes.

He found himself smiling at her as she joyfully helped the children interpret the clues to find the treasure. *She is definitely still fine.* Riveted, he took in her mustard, midi pleated-waist skirt and cream colored sleeveless blouse. By the looks of things, he was definitely involved in the treasure hunt...in hot pursuit of Gabrielle. And, from the reaction of his body, the pleasure was all his.

Suddenly, his eyebrows drew together in a serious gaze. *What am I thinking?* Aggravated, he wanted to slap himself for eyeing her so excessively, for even thinking about her in that way. *Better stop this foolishness*, he cautioned himself, concentrating on the game. Even then, his body had other ideas, which he deliberately ignored.

An hour later, everyone returned to the living room, happy but totally exhausted from the treasure hunt and other games. Princess Angelica was the happiest, squealing with delight as she opened her many gifts. Gabrielle sat close by, writing down the names of the givers and the contents of each gift as Vivian read the card that was attached.

"And, last but not least," Vivian announced, "There is a gift from Uncle Blake. It's too heavy so you will have to move from your seat, Angelica."

Angelica looked around wildly for the gift but could not find it. She grinned at Blake who was sitting with her father and the other adults behind the children who were still seated in a semi-circle. "Where is it?" she said gleefully.

"Come on!" Vivian motioned to her.

Angelica held on to her mother's hand, excited to be led to her final gift. All the children attempted to follow suit.

"No need to move everyone," Vivian said to the group. "It's right here. Take your seats."

And the children did so, barely able to contain their enthusiasm as they anticipated the next gift.

Angelica tugged on her mother's hand, whispered in her ear before turning to face her guests. "I just want to say thanks to my favorite aunt, Aunt Gabrielle for her many gifts." She smiled at Gabrielle, and then waved her hand from her head to her toe. "She is responsible for all of this, and my gown which I took off." She ran across the room and hugged Gabrielle, who was now sitting a chair away from Blake. "Thanks, Aunt Gabrielle."

"You're welcome, dear!" Gabrielle hugged her tightly before releasing her.

"Uncle Blake!" she squealed, giving him a quick hug before racing towards her dad.

James had moved the chair that Angelica was sitting in to reveal a huge box, wrapped in pink candy striped paper. Angelica attacked the box immediately, ripping the paper away. Her dad held the box steady as she did so. When she finally opened the box, she let out a shriek and ran to hug Uncle Blake again before racing back to the gift to reveal a Barbie bike.

"Thanks, Uncle Blake," she grinned at him. "I love it."

Blake smiled at her. "You're welcome, my Earth Angel."

The rest of the party remained uneventful and soon everyone was on their way home.

With Blake's and James' help, Angelica had moved all her gifts including her bike to her bedroom. She was clearly enjoying her gifts since she had not returned to the living room.

Blake stayed back along with Gabrielle to help with the cleanup and Vivian and James were totally grateful.

"We are almost back to normal," Vivian said clutching James' hand as she surveyed the living room.

"Almost," Gabrielle agreed from across the room.

"We'll take it from here." Vivian's gaze shifted from Gabrielle to Blake. "Thanks so much, guys."

"You all got more work out of me than the law allows," Blake teased. "Nevertheless, you're welcome."

A ripple of laughter erupted in the room.

"We are willing to pay," Vivian countered still grinning.

"Will send you a bill," Blake quipped chuckling. He glanced in Gabrielle's direction. "Ready?" he asked.

"Yes!" Gabrielle responded, moving to the sofa to retrieve her purse. She hugged Vivian who hugged her back tightly.

"God bless you," Vivian murmured in her ears before hugging Blake.

Gabrielle proceeded to hug James. "Have a good evening," he told her.

Gabrielle waited, watching as Blake said goodbye to James.

They all walked to the door and James opened it. "See you soon!" he said, his arms around Vivian.

"Bye!" Blake and Gabrielle responded in unison.

CHAPTER 15

FROM THE HEART

The sound of the front door closing echoed in Gabrielle's ear as she walked with Blake in silence towards their cars. *I wished Vivian and James had walked us to our cars*, she mused. She glanced at Blake but he was looking intently ahead. *Is he trying to avoid looking at me?* She wrinkled her nose disapprovingly before brushing the thought aside, deciding to be positive. She opened her mouth to speak, but then closed it when she realized she didn't have anything to say...no words anyway that would improve the somewhat awkward silence.

The evening breeze felt cool against her face as she gathered her thoughts and began to formulate what she was going to say to generate conversation. She nibbled on her lips as they stopped at her car. "Thanks for what you did at the party. I appreciate that you didn't make it more uncomfortable for me."

Blake nodded looking towards the door of her car as if waiting for her to get in.

"Blake, please," she said passionately, "I miss you. I'm sorry for what I-"

A flash of displeasure lit his countenance and he tried to tamp it down. "Gabby, not now," he told her in a formal tone, hoping to convey the message he was not in the mood for drama.

She flipped her hair from her face and gave him an exasperated look as she questioned agitatedly. "If not now Blake, when? Are you going to pretend it didn't happen?"

His eyebrows drew together in a severe gaze and he did not respond for a moment. He was busy holding back the choice words he wanted to yell at her. "Pretend?" he echoed, barely restraining himself. "Get in your car. I need to go."

She frowned. "Are you seeing someone?"

A look of incredulity crossed his features. "And, what if I am?" Annoyance edged his voice.

She searched his defiant eyes, then her shoulders drooped and her eyes hit the floor in defeat. "Are you seeing Zoe?" she asked quietly, feeling tightness in her throat. *Please God, not Zoe...not anyone*. The very idea of Blake and Zoe made her grind her teeth.

He felt like saying something cruel to hurt her but he didn't have the heart to. "I'm not seeing anyone," he stated. "You of all people should know I'm not like that."

She let out a long sigh of relief and when she looked at him, she felt tears springing up behind her eyelids. "Can we talk about us, sometime?"

"Talk?" Blake looked away from her, hiding his eyes which were smoldering with resentment. *Geeze! What is it about this woman that I have always allowed her to get under my skin?* "There's really nothing to talk about," he said sharply.

His response seemed to hang in the air before piercing her heart. Her chest tightened. This was not the response she'd hoped to hear or wanted to hear. *Is he that heartless? Is this how we are going to live? There is plenty to talk about.* She looked at his proud posture clearly indicating their conversation was over.

"Okay," she muttered, totally defeated.

She wanted to tell him exactly what she thought, but the words lodged in her throat. Instead, tears of hurt and frustration rolled down her cheeks as she entered her car and started the ignition. She did not look at him as she spoke, her hands gripped the steering wheel and she could barely see in front of her. "Have a good evening," she managed to say. She attempted to close the door but he held on to it.

"You cannot drive in this condition," he said, hating the concern in his voice.

"I'm okay," she said mopping her eyes with a wad of tissue from a box in the glove compartment. But the more, she mopped her eyes, the more tears poured down her cheeks.

"I'm not leaving until you pull yourself together," he said, not releasing the door.

Gabrielle dried the remainder of her tears, willing herself, but unable to come to terms with his feelings about meeting with her. "I'm okay," she insisted, looking straight ahead. "I'm going to leave now."

Blake let out a jagged sigh then dragged an impatient hand through his hair. "I just can't right now, Gabby."

Tearful eyes met his. "Are you going to punish me for the rest of my life?"

He gave her a long, hard stare and his features turned stone cold. "Punish you? You did this to yourself, to us," he said accusingly. "All I did was love you."

She gasped at the bitterness in his voice. "I'm sorry. So sorry," she sobbed, gulping for air as a sharp pain penetrated her heart. "I don't know what else to do to show you that I'm sorry."

He stood there, clutching the door. *You destroyed our marriage and I should welcome you back with open arms. Really?* His lips thinned into a straight line.

Gabrielle grabbed the door trying to pull it out of his hands but he refused to let it go. She collapsed on the steering wheel and wept even more.

He turned off the ignition, closed the door and marched back to the front door of the house. *Why didn't I leave after the party was over? I wouldn't be in this predicament.* He let out a shallow breath and rang the doorbell. *God help me!*

James appeared with Vivian in tow.

"Hey," James greeted him, while Vivian watched nervously behind him.

"If you don't mind, I'll return for my car later. I'm going to drive Gabby home," Blake said in a stoic voice.

"Sure! Is Gabrielle alright?" James asked.

Blake paused momentarily, wondering how to respond. "She'll be alright. It's best I take her home."

"I could drive your car and-"

"I don't want to trouble you. You've all had a long day."

"No trouble at all," Vivian added, her head bobbing from side to side. "A twenty minute drive will do us no harm. What are friends for?"

"Okay. Thanks," Blake said. "Here's my key."

"I will drive your car and Vivian will drive hers," James suggested.

"That will work," Vivian said, moving away. "Let me get the princess."

"Thanks again!" Blake said. "I'm going ahead of you."

"Okay. We're right behind you," James said, before closing the door.

Blake walked back to Gabrielle's car. *She did this to herself. Why is she making me out to be a villain?* He found Gabby still crying her heart out against the steering wheel.

"Gabby," he called out after opening the door, "you need to move over and let me drive."

"No," she responded, looking at him with tear-stained cheeks. "I'll drive-"

"You cannot drive in this condition."

Instinctively, she stiffened. "As if you care whether I live or die," she countered in disdain. She swung her legs out of the car and tried to grab her keys from his hand.

"Stop it," he rasped impatiently.

"I'm not a child," she hollered, tears streaming down her face. "Give me my keys."

He sighed, picked her up and cradled her like a child in his arms as he walked around the car.

She was too stunned to protest.

He opened the passenger door, placed her on the seat and strapped her in.

"I'm not a child you know," he heard her mutter as he slid behind the steering wheel.

She cried quietly, the whole way home, her shoulders quivering at times.

Blake did not utter a word until he pulled into the garage. "Stay in the car," he told her, before exiting to collect his car key from James.

"Thanks, Man," Blake said to James.

"You're welcome, Brother." James hopped out of Blake's car and handed him the key. "Viv will literally kill me if I don't ask," he said in a quiet tone. "Will Gabrielle be alright? Does Viv need to stay with her for a while?"

"Yes, she'll be alright. No need for Vivian to stay with her," Blake responded. "Thanks for your concern. I am too," he heard himself say. "I'll make sure she's okay before I leave."

"Great! Well take care, Brother," James said.

"Thanks again, James."

"No problem. See you soon."

They parted company and when James hopped into the car with Vivian and Angelica, Blake waved goodbye to them.

He walked back to Gabrielle's car and closed the garage door before opening the car door for her. She sighed, clutched her purse to her chest then got out of the car.

Blake closed the car door behind her and they walked to the house door.

She took out her key and was having difficulty inserting it in the lock so he came up behind her and took it from her hand then proceeded to open the door.

She could feel his breath on her neck, and all she could think about was being in his arms. She needed him. Throwing caution to the wind, she turned and threw her arms around his shoulder. All the emotions that she'd suppressed since their separation were on full display and she clung to him burying her head in his neck.

He tensed, then swung an arm around her waist and lifted her through the door to the living room. He could feel the fluttering of her heart, but it was the warmth of her breath against his neck that threatened to derail him. He quickly placed her on the ground before the sofa and relaxed his grip on her waist.

But Gabrielle did not let go. *This is where I belong,* she told herself. A feeling of unimaginable warmth flushed her body and she closed her eyes, delighting in the feel of his body against hers.

He felt the familiar heightened excitement in their bodies and emergency bells went off in his brain. *Stop her now or there's no looking back.*

"Need to go," he told her, unclasping her hands from around his neck. He let out a thankful sigh, extremely grateful that he was still in control of his unbridled emotions.

She plopped down on the sofa as he dropped her keys on the coffee table. "Blake, please, can we talk about us," she begged.

He turned away and headed towards the front door, unable to bear the desperation in her voice. "I have to go. I'll catch up with you."

A flutter of pain gripped her heart and she sprang off the sofa. "Blake, please!"

The anguish in her voice stopped him in his tracks and he turned to face her, his hand holding the door knob. Silence passed between them as he considered his next words. "Don't know if I can handle what you have to say," he told her quietly. "Pray for me," he added, opening the door.

"I will," she said.

"Goodnight."

"Night," she responded.

He closed the door behind him.

She waited until she heard the distinctive roar of the engine before moving away from the door. Her shoulders sagged in defeat, and she brushed away the single tear that slid down her cheek, as she made her way back to the living room. She was having a hard time being anything other than disappointed.

CHAPTER 16

FULL DISCLOSURE

Almost a week later, Gabrielle clasped her hands and murmured a quick prayer in the living room when she heard the doorbell. After taking a few steps she stopped and nervously glanced down at herself, trusting she was appropriately dressed and ready for the daunting task ahead. *Breathe, she encouraged herself.*

When she reached the front door, she looked through the peephole and saw Blake standing on the patio. His gorgeous dark brown eyes seemed to stare back at her. Not surprising, he was right on time.

Glancing at the floor, she steadied herself. *Please grant me favor, Lord. Turn his heart towards me again.* Placing a slight smile on her face, she opened the door.

"Blake, come in!" She hoped she added enough warmth to her greeting.

"Hey, Gabby," he said, stepping inside and closing the door behind him.

She eyed him. "I thought you had your key."

"I do, but I didn't want to intrude."

"Not at all. Please don't feel that way." She threw her hair behind her back, and then motioned with her hands, "Let's talk in the living room."

Blake followed her, attempting to ignore her incredibly beautiful carriage ahead of him. He couldn't help but stare. Her sleeveless denim dress fitted smoothly over her curves. A perfect fit. She looked simply incredible at thirty-five years old.

"Would you like something to drink?" she asked softly.

"No. Thanks. I'm good." He took a seat on the small sofa, his long torso reclining luxuriously.

155

She tried to read his expression but found nothing. "Let me get something for myself," she told him, moving to the kitchen. Although he'd rejected her first request for a meeting, she'd decided to call him again, thinking, *"...if I perish, I perish!"* So, she was pleasantly surprised when he'd agreed to do so.

Sitting in the living room, Blake suddenly felt nostalgic. He shook his head, reminding himself to stay focused since he had no intention of moving back home. The rattling of a teacup brought him back to the present as Gabrielle entered the living room and sat on the large sofa across from him.

Gabrielle tilted her head and met Blake's gaze. *Lord, help me! He is giving me nothing.* "Blake," she began softly, "Thanks for coming."

He nodded, his expression still masked.

"I wanted you know that I'm sorry for what I did to you and our marriage." She paused, hoping to hear something from him but nothing came. He continued to look at her, his expression unreadable. For a brief moment a feeling of apprehension shot through her and she nibbled on her lips then decided to press on. She'd come too far. Placing her teacup on the coffee table, she clasped her hands on her lap and exhaled deeply. "Please forgive me for what I've done." Still, nothing came from him. "I love you," she whispered, struggling to hold his gaze. "I am hoping that you would still want to continue our marriage."

Continue our marriage! Continue our marriage, echoed in Blake's ears as he stared blankly at her, tensing himself so he wouldn't shake his head in disbelief. In all honesty, he hadn't known what to expect when he'd agreed to meet with her. Last weekend when she'd requested the meeting, he felt unprepared to hear her out. Plus, he was annoyed that she had the nerve to ask. She had no right pestering him for a meeting, no right to even ask for a

156

meeting. How could she try to seek closure when he was not yet ready? He should have been the one asking for closure.

But the more he prayed and thought about meeting with Gabrielle, the more he knew it was the right thing to do. He and Gabrielle needed to talk. Perhaps, just to clear the air and press on with their individual lives. Plus, he had no intention of dragging the issue between them into the New Year. So, he asked the Lord for the right timing and to prepare their hearts for the meeting. But the Lord moved quicker than he'd anticipated. Gabrielle had called a few days later to request a meeting for that Friday evening. They had both taken the day off from work - which was somewhat torturous for him - so they could meet early afternoon.

Thinking that the silence between them had stretched long enough, he responded, "I have forgiven you. That's why I'm here, but," he lifted a brow, "with regards to continuing our marriage, I'm not there and honestly, don't know if I'll ever be."

A strangled cry escaped her. "Blake, please! Please don't say that."

She stood and moved away from the sofa she was sitting in to try and calm herself as despair warred against hope to take the lead in her internal struggle. Deep down, a part of her wanted to believe that he still loved her and wanted their marriage to continue. "I would do anything to restore our marriage," she pleaded, clasping her hands and looking earnestly at him.

He pursed his lips while looking at her. He certainly was not there to torture her. In fact, a small part of him wanted to reach out and comfort her.

"Your infidelity shattered my trust in you," he stated quietly. "And, I have no desire to live a tortured life every time you are not in my presence."

157

Her eyes flashed with disappointment and anguish laced her voice as she responded. "I made a mistake, a mistake Blake, one that is threatening to cost me everything I treasure. I never stopped loving you."

"I can't, Gabby. Don't know if I ever will. Just the thought of opening up myself to you again scares me."

The knots of sadness and disappointment forming in his heart, reminded him of all he'd been through. He exhaled deeply then stood up and moved away from the sofa to stand near to her. "You've hurt me. Hurt me, real badly," he stated, gritting his teeth. "At one stage, I thought I was going insane. I was just hoping to make it to the next day. The unbearable pain in my heart would just not go away." He stuffed his hands into the pockets of his pants to hide how much they were trembling. "You pulled the rug from under my feet, brought me to my knees, and," he paused to gather himself, "and left my life spinning out of control." He rubbed his chin thoughtfully as he returned to the sofa. "I didn't realize how much my life was wrapped up in you."

Gabrielle listened quietly, eyes downcast, knowing that he had to get it out.

"Words cannot describe the pain I'd experienced. I didn't even know my heart could hurt, much less hurt so much. The sense of loss I felt was unbelievable. I lost something deeply personal and my spirit was crushed in a way that I cannot begin to explain." He looked at her motionless stature. "I was joined to you then severed from you in the," his voice broke, "the cruelest way."

He sat still for a moment, collecting himself.

In the quietness of the moment, she returned to the sofa. She knew he was not finished so she remained silent.

"We had a special connection, a rare connection," Blake continued in a professorial tone. "We had the ability to look in each other's soul because of our Christ centered

158

lives. I loved my life and who I was becoming with you in my life. And, you led me to believe you felt the same way too." He looked at her. "It is still difficult for me to understand why you slept with Larry. I can't erase that out of my mind. Our love was great, but that was just the appetizer. For me, the main course was our connection to God and when that special triangle was ripped apart, I was torn to pieces."

With his elbows on his knees, he clasped his hands together under his chin as if in prayer. "Thank God for Bishop Clandon. He has been a tower of strength. I'm still trying to find my way through the leading of the Holy Spirit," he acknowledged quietly.

"I'm sorry," Gabrielle responded softly. "I never intended to hurt you. I wish I could undo what I did. I didn't tell you about Larry, even though he coerced me, because I felt that I was partly to be blamed for what happened. I should not have allowed him to massage my shoulder...to touch my body in any way. I let my guard down because I was extremely tired." She paused to look at him but he had reclined in the sofa and closed his eyes. "Blake, I'm sorry. Please understand I never meant to hurt you."

For a moment, Blake wished things were different between them. Although he tried to prepare for all she had to say, he was hoping that she would not expound on what actually happened between her and Larry Kanate. He didn't know if he could handle it.

And, he had a few choice words for that conniving Kanate if he ever laid eyes on him. Not for lack of trying. He even thought of doing a drive-by. But wait, he did do a drive-by... three times but had no way to get through the electronic gate at Larry and Rozene's lavish French-style mansion. He had even rehearsed the dialogue between himself and Kanate, many times in his head. For sure, it would have gone down between them, ending with Kanate being knocked out.

In fact, up to two months ago, against the warnings of the Holy Spirit, he'd pressed the intercom button at the huge wrought iron electronic entrance gate to Larry and Rozene's home. When he did not get a response, he'd marched back to his car, and after sliding behind the steering wheel, he'd spent a few minutes glaring at the gate. As he drove away, Blake heard the Holy Spirit impress on his spirit, "You are not that kind of person. You are better than that." *Now that's the truth.* But, he still wanted Larry to pay for what he'd done to Gabrielle.

Blake gazed at Gabrielle. *Where was the confident, I-have-it all-together woman whom I married?* The helplessness that surrounded her was all new to him...almost puzzling.

"Blake," Gabrielle swallowed hard then looked away, "there's something I've wanted to share with you for the longest while."

He became still, giving her his attention.

"I was ashamed to tell you because it had caused me many sleepless nights, but no more," she declared. "It's the reason why I'm so protective of children and why I didn't think I would be a great mom."

Blake softened. "You know you can tell me anything."

"I know but fear kept me bound. But, I'm good now." With that Gabrielle released herself. "Before we got married, I'd told you I was not a virgin. What I didn't tell you was how I lost my virginity." A flash of pain shot through her eyes. "I was raped."

Blake sucked in his breath as he absorbed the words he didn't anticipate hearing. "RAPED! Why didn't you...?"

160

"I was sixteen when it happened," Gabrielle voice caught. "It happened at my cousin's wedding. Jesse Lowery was my neighbor. We…"

Raped! Blake wrestled with muddled emotions as Gabrielle poured out her heart, tearfully recounting her story. A chilling sense of powerlessness invaded his entire being. *How could this have happened to her? Why didn't she tell me?* Now, he felt like physically hurting both Jesse Lowery and Larry Kanate.

Gabrielle's tearful panting brought him back to reality.

"I got pregnant and lost the child. I felt unworthy to have another child because I didn't want to carry the baby, although after a while, I grew to love the fact that I was carrying life within me." She wiped away her tears with her hands. Her eyes reflecting the pain she'd carried for so long.

Blake's heart was filled with compassion as he watched her.

"I had always felt guilty," she said, "fearful that someone would find out my dirty little secret. So I kept silent. And while I kept silent, pretending that I wasn't raped, the hardness around my heart grew into a fortress." She exhaled. "Unconsciously, I felt obligated to protect children, trying to save them from the cruelty in this world." She attempted a smile. "I thank God that I've worked through my issues and I've been released and set free from all of that."

Tears filled his eyes as he listened. "Gabby, I'm sorry," he said softly, moving to join her on the sofa. He touched her arm briefly, all choked up. "You've been through so much."

She eyed him hesitantly while raising her hand to indicate she had more to say. "When Larry started to…"

161

Her voice broke and her face crumbled as she choked back a sob.

Blake reached out a hand to touch her shoulder but she shifted to avoid his hand.

She needed to say what was on her heart, despite the heaviness that was slowly building in her chest. She began again. "When Larry started to force himself on me, I froze. It took me back to the time when I was being raped by Jesse. I felt like I was suspended in time and place, in a horrible, horrible nightmare." Her lips began to tremble and she pursed them as tears rushed in. For a few minutes, she said nothing, until she regained control of her emotions. "I just stood there, watching myself being sexually assaulted for a second time in my life. A second time!" Her disbelieving eyes met his, but in a matter of seconds, they glazed over with sadness. "I urged myself to scream, to tell Larry to stop…to fight him. But, I was too stunned. Simply rendered speechless; my heart hammering at what seemed like a billion beats per second." Tears broke free and she allowed them to escape. "It was terrifying," she said unsteadily.

Blake watched as the words escaped her lips. Instinctively, he wanted to comfort her…although bolting for the door did run across his mind. It was a lot to take in and process. He felt as though he was at war with himself - a part of him wanting to comfort her and the other part wanting him to protect his heart. Nevertheless, wanting to ease her fears was hitting him harder. What she'd experienced wasn't a nightmare, it actually happened…not once but twice.

He drew in a deep breath and then slowly released it, attempting to settle his muddled emotions. Yet he continued to ooze compassion, understanding, and…love. Compassion was at the forefront and he allowed it to roam freely in his heart. He was comfortable with that. That was the only emotion he knew was right for a moment such as this. Only a heartless human being could have felt nothing in this moment. He didn't want to say anything, didn't want to ask anything. All he wanted to do was hold her until the pain in her heart vanished. But, she was not giving him the chance and that was slightly unnerving. And if her tears didn't stop, he was afraid he would start hollering too. So, he was glad when she spoke again.

"I thought I had put the rape behind me," she said quietly. "Thought I'd buried it away, forever." She clutched her hands and gazed at the floor. "Blake, I'm sorry. I had no intention of hurting you."

He almost didn't hear her choked words.

She lifted weepy eyes to his then lowered her gaze. "You have rebuilt my faith in men. As you know, I didn't have a father figure in my life and being sexually abused had caused me to distrust men."

His features softened and he knew the moment was right. So, he reached over and pulled her in his arms, wrapping her in the 'blanket of care' he created. He wanted to wipe away all her woes - the rape, the miscarriage, and the pain of their separation. Hugging her closely, he murmured words of comfort as she clung to his chest, weeping quietly.

CHAPTER 17

FROM DEEP WITHIN

Fifteen minutes later, against the wishes of her body, Gabrielle heaved herself from Blake's chest. *I won't make a big deal of this. He's just trying to comfort me.* She gazed at him momentarily taking in the compassion in his eyes. Her full disclosure about her past had impacted him and softened his heart towards her.

Hope surged in her heart.

She tucked strands of hair behind her ears, then said almost formally, "Excuse me for a moment," before walking towards what use to be their bedroom.

Blake's eyes followed her, staring at her body and out of nowhere a leisurely smile of appreciation spread across his face followed by a flicker of surprise as his body responded to his thoughts. He stood up abruptly and walked to inspect a painting on the wall, feeling almost guilty for having sensuous thoughts at a time like this.

He glanced around the spacious contemporary living room, knowing every corner. The lightest shade of mint green covered the walls. It was still decorated as he'd recalled - The three off-white overstuffed leather sofas with a nice pop of lime green, red, and black cushions were strategically placed in the center of the room to surround the stylish rectangular black coffee table that was sitting in the center of the huge lime green fur rug on the pristine wooden floor. Decorative accents and eye-catching ornaments in a variety of dark and bright hues added extra depth and dimension. Pure elegance resulted whether light poured through the huge windows or came from the beautiful crystal chandelier that was hanging in the center of the ceiling.

Silently, Blake returned to the sofa and sat watching as Gabrielle entered the room. Her movements seemed odd, slightly tentative and he noticed that she was carrying a bag in one hand. She sat slightly away from him, reached into the bag and pulled out her 'comfort' box and placed it on her lap. She gently pulled on the twine and the bow on top of the box cover slid away. She looked Blake in the eye. "I always smile when you call this my 'comfort' box but now I realize it was not really a 'comfort' box."

He held his curiosity and allowed her to finish.

"It contains all the stuff for the child that I'd lost. I know the baby was only a few weeks old but I felt very responsible for the miscarriage. I thought maybe if I'd embraced the pregnancy sooner, then my body would not have rejected the baby. So I kept all that I'd accumulated for her so I would remember that great things can also come out of unpleasant situations." She sighed softly, staring at the floor. "I thought it was going to be a girl."

Blake covered her hand with his. "It's okay. God is all about healing broken places in our lives. You were raped so I have utmost respect for you wanting to carry the child." He smiled softly at her. "You would have been a great mother."

She gave him a shy smile, conscious that his hand was still on top of hers. "Thank you. Didn't think I would, but Vivian was my cheerleader in that regard."

Blake squeezed her hand before letting go. "You will make a great mom, someday," he reaffirmed. Her mouth curled into a smile and he watched as her eyes lit up.

"Thanks," she said softly, before lifting the cover on the 'comfort' box and dropping the twine in it. *My box of memories!* Her smile faded, replaced by a solemn expression as a lump lodged in her throat. *Life sure doesn't always go as planned.*

"Are you okay?" Blake asked, sensing the change in her mood.

"Yes," she responded, determined to move forward. She closed the 'comfort' box and positioned it between her hands. "I want to burn the contents," she told him. "I brought a large steel pan to burn them in the backyard."

"Do you really want to?"

She nodded. "Yes. Can you help me?"

"Sure!" He wasn't sure if he should be a part of the burning ritual but he knew she needed support at this juncture in her life.

She led the way to the backyard.

He stood silently behind her as she poured kerosene oil from a small bottle on firewood in the pan, and then lit it.

I'm ready now, Gabrielle thought. Her throat constricted and she swallowed hard, before turning to Blake who was holding the 'comfort' box with both hands. She laid her hands on top of the 'comfort' box for a moment before tracing the edges with her fingers. Her 'comfort' box had been with her for almost twenty years. *Can I let it go?* Old memories - emptiness, rejection, and loss - rushed in, and doubt began to gather in her mind like dark clouds covering a blue sky. Her chest tightened as fear washed through her, but she refused to give into it. It was time. She'd made the decision and now she intended to follow through with it. She took a few quick breaths and blew them out.

Blake waited patiently, a bittersweet sense of pride forming in his chest. From Gabrielle's expression, he knew the task at hand was not easy for her.

Lifting the cover, Gabrielle reached into the 'comfort' box and grabbed a hold of a bunch of papers. "These are letters that I'd written during my pregnancy and after I'd lost the baby." She glanced at each before throwing them in the fire. Next, she dropped the twine into the fire where it sizzled and burned.

Blake sent up a silent prayer for her, knowing that she had to do this ritual and do it in her own way.

She held up the sonogram. "It's almost faded," she said softly, before dropping it in the pan and watching it being swallowed up by the flames.

Her eyes washed with pain. "The day I did the ultrasound was the day when I acknowledged that I was carrying precious life within me."

He touched her shoulder lightly in an attempt to comfort her as she reached into the box for the final item. Tears trickled down her cheeks and he quickly closed the box and circled her waist with his free hand.

She wiped her eyes with the back of her hands, but tears continued to stream down her face. "Thank you," she said, moving out of their embrace. Strangely, she did not want his touch.

"Vivian gave me this teddy bear to secure her position as godmother," she told him. She kissed the teddy bear before tossing it into the flames.

"And she would have made a great godmother," Blake responded quietly, not touching her. He'd sensed she didn't want to be touched.

She nodded without meeting his gaze. "Forgot to burn the box," she muttered, agitatedly.

"The fire is still blazing," he encouraged.

She took the box from him and threw it in the fire. As the bright red flames sprung up, he pulled her away and unconsciously into his arms. For a moment, time stood still as they drank in the all too familiar scent of each other, their hearts seemingly pounding in sync. She shuddered, leaning into him and he wrapped his arms around her waist, knowing the whole ordeal had been too much for her.

"It's going to be alright," he murmured, kissing the top of her head.

Suddenly, she sprang out of his arms and released a crackling maniacal laugh, before facing him, with hands akimbo. "Alright?" She glared at him, an unending stream of tears running down her cheeks.

For a moment, he stood there not knowing what to do. Then, he reached for her hand. "Gabby-"

"Don't touch me!" she yelled hysterically, her eyes blazing. "You, you…hate me," she sobbed loudly. "You hate…me." She backed away from him, her expression filled with torture. "I have no one! No one! Not my baby! Not you! I've lost everything I treasured." She ran towards the back door then whirled around. "It doesn't matter now. Nothing matters now. No matter how hard I tried, how long I prayed, nothing will bring you back. I've accomplished nothing."

Blake edged closer to her, noticing that she was shaking. "Let's go inside," he encouraged, steeling himself as tears threatened.

She wrapped her arms around her body. "Leave me alone," she croaked out between sobs. "You said you would always love me," she hunched her shoulders, turning slightly away from him, "but you, you only want to love me when you think I'm perfect," she squeezed out between short gasps of breath.

He touched her shoulder and she shrugged off his hand, another bout of tears spilling from her eyes.

"You don't love me!" she accused him, bowing over as if the thought was too much to handle. And then, fresh revelation hit and she jerked upright, staring blindly. "He… doesn't… love… me!" she said slowly, desperately wanting her heart to hear and understand.

Blake blinked rapidly in an attempt to get rid of the tears that were forming as she unleashed her emotions. "Gabby, stop-"

She made a loud gulp, lifting a hand to stop him. Her eyes were swollen. "You look at me with judgment and scorn. I look at myself that way too because I am ashamed," she paused to catch a quick breath, "Ashamed of what I did."

She swayed and he grabbed her by the waist and pulled her to him. "Don't touch me," she said, hammering his chest with her hands. He held her hands and she dropped her head on his chest, exhausted from her fight.

"I'm sooo ashamed," she lamented between sobs. "Ashamed that I made another man touch me in that way. Oh my God! Oh my God!" She yanked herself away from him. "I ruined my life."

He reached for her but she stepped further away. "You're making yourself sick."

But, she droned on, "I make people talk about us. I brought shame to our household." Her eyes widened. "No wonder you look at me like..." In the next breath, she grabbed a hold of the back door, gasping for air. Her body swayed and she threw a hand wildly in the air trying to find him as her legs began to buckle.

And instantly, he caught her just as everything was vanishing into varying shades of gray. He held her against him and she tried to cling to him but there was no strength in her arms. "Breathe," he told her, as she gaped at him. "Breathe slowly. That's it," he encouraged her as if communicating with a small child.

When he felt she was out of the danger zone, he reached forward, pulled the door open, and then lifted her in his arms. He stepped inside and heard the door close behind him.

He carried her to the living room and placed her on the largest sofa, but she was shaking so much he had to hold her in his arms for a few minutes.

"I need to get you something to drink," he told her, leaning her against the back of the sofa.

"Wa-water," she murmured, her eyes half-lidded. She felt dizzy and spacey as if she was floating in oblivion.

"Okay."

He walked to the kitchen, scanned the refrigerator and decided that water would probably be the best option. When he returned to the living room, she was stretched out on the sofa. He placed the bottle of water on the coffee table and touched her shoulders, encouraging her to sit up. She stared at him blankly, and then reached out a hand for assistance. He helped her up into a sitting position then took the water from the coffee table and sat beside her. His hand circling her waist, he gently fed her the water.

"Drink slowly," he told her.

After sipping a little of the water, she shook her head, indicating that she had had enough. Her head was both pounding and the room seemed to be tilting, heightening her dizziness.

He waited for a few minutes, hugging her shoulder while she leaned on him before encouraging her to drink some more. She sipped more of the water then he placed the bottle on the ground beside the sofa.

Knowing he couldn't leave her in that state, he pushed backwards to the corner of the sofa, swung one of his legs behind her back, while the other rested on the ground, then pulled her onto his chest. She closed her eyes and buried her face in his chest.

She was still shuddering so he hugged her waist and her shoulder to keep her in place. He felt her silent tears, dampening his shirt but it didn't matter. All that mattered was that she needed to cry. No words were necessary. He just held her because she needed it...and because he wanted to.

When he heard her breathing steadily, he knew she had fallen asleep. He quietly wiped away his own tears and whispered a prayer, thanking God for His grace on her life.

At the end of the prayer, he reclined deeper on the sofa so that she could lie even more comfortably on his chest. And when she stirred, arching her body closer to his, he gently caressed her hair to relax her. Within a few minutes, the tension in her body thawed and she fell into a deeper sleep.

For an hour, his mind rehearsed all that she had told him. Glancing at the gold wedding band on his hand, he sucked in a deep breath. It struck him forcefully. They were right back where their fight started... on the sofa...in the living room.

Gabrielle felt the increase in his heart rate and tilted her face towards his. "How long have I been sleeping?" she murmured. *I have not slept this comfortable in a long while.*

His breathing quickened as the warmth of her breath grazed his neck. How he longed for the sweetness emanating from their bodies. "Not long, perhaps a little over an hour," he managed to get out.

The deep huskiness in his voice caused her heart to leap...and she wanted to take that leap. Her hands moved around his neck and she ran her fingers through the hair at the back of his head, tugging on the strands. She took a quick breath, and was glad she did, because her nostrils were filled with his male scent. She'd always loved the way he smelled. *I love everything about him,* she acknowledged, sighing in contentment. She always felt safe and totally wonderful around him.

Blake's entire body hummed with pleasurable energy and he knew he had to break free before it was too late. His body wanted hers but his heart was not ready to commit. Raking a hand through his hair, he sighed then cleared his throat. "Are you feeling better?"

Gabrielle pulled away from him, reading his sigh as rejection of her affection. Nevertheless, she knew from his physical response to her, that he was not as immune as he pretended to be. "Yes. Thanks so much for asking. And, thanks for listening," she countered while fixing her hair then straightening her clothes.

Blake saw the disappointment in her eyes, but knew he couldn't trust himself with her at this point. She looked well but she was in a fragile state. He didn't want them to do anything that they would both regret.

"Gabby, I…" he began, ready to explain that he was not shunning her.

"It's okay." She looked him in the eye. "Really, it is. No explanation necessary." She rose from the sofa but not before she saw a glimmer of love in his eyes. However, it was gone in a moment. "Let me show you out."

"Would you like me to make you something to eat?" he asked, pulling his muscular body to full height.

Her body quivered in appreciation. "That's alright. I'll make something later," she said, moving ahead of him.

"Okay."

Blake glanced at her erect posture ahead of him as they walked in silence to the door. He wished he had something to say, something that would make her smile again.

At the door, she stepped aside and he hesitated just for a moment before turning the door knob.

"For the record, I don't hate you," he told her quietly on the patio. "Have a good night."

For a moment he thought she might cry then her face softened and she reached up and brushed her lips against his cheek. "I know you don't. Have a good night, too." And before he could respond, she stepped through the door, closed it behind her and leaned against it. *He doesn't hate me, but, he didn't say that he loves me.* Nevertheless, she felt free.

Blake stood for a few minutes on the patio as an emotional war raged within. He let out a ragged sigh. Exhaling deeply, he moved on, knowing he was not ready.

CHAPTER 18

NOTHING TO LOSE

"Glad you wore this amazing color," Vivian told Gabrielle, inspecting her cute fuchsia pink dress in the sanctuary at church. It was Wednesday night and they had just attended Bible Study.

Gabrielle regarded her curiously, since Vivian had picked her up at home and gave her a ride to church. "Glad I could add to your joy. Is there something I should know?"

"I did you a favor," Vivian said ignoring her monotone.

Gabrielle eyed her suspiciously. "Why do I have a bad feeling about this?"

"It's all good. In fact, you'll love it." Vivian patted her back. "Blake is taking you home."

Gabrielle gasped. "Viv, No! I told you I haven't heard from him since our meeting. Four whole days passed and I haven't heard a single word from him. Not a single word. And, I feel like I'm going cuckoo because my mind keeps circling around the same thought - What if he decides to divorce me now that he knows my past?"

"Stop thinking crazy. I told you he'd called me and told me, little old me, to keep an eye on you," Vivian encouraged. "You'll be alright. I've got a great feeling about this."

"Of course someone just must keep an eye on me. Didn't I tell you about our last encounter? He must have thought I was a raging lunatic, a basket case. I was way out there."

"And, for that you got to spread out on his chest. Unbelievable!" Vivian grinned at her stern, unyielding face.

"Right! Not feeling proud of myself about that either." She eyed Vivian. "He should have been the one keeping an eye on me. He was the witness to my disturbing behavior."

"Girlfriend, I told you he said he had to make an emergency run out of town."

"So his phone doesn't work?" She pursed her lips. "Let me stop harassing you."

"Yes, please! And remember you are joining us for Christmas dinner." Vivian lifted a hand as Gabrielle began to protest.

"I told you, I'll think about it," Gabrielle said.

"It sounded like a yes to me. My family is expecting you on Saturday, Madam. And, don't disappoint your goddaughter."

"So, you're just going to threaten me? Why don't you throw in a little arm twisting too?"

"That can be arranged," Vivian said playfully reaching for her arm. "FYI, Blake is spending Christmas weekend with his parents."

"Good for him."

"And, right about now, he's heading our way."

"Help me, Lord," Gabrielle muttered adjusting her posture in preparation to see Blake. "You will pay for this."

"Stop it," Vivian giggled. "This is not the mafia."

"For your sake, you better hope it's not," she said in a low tone sensing Blake was nearby. She turned to face Blake and her eyes widened involuntarily, her expression asking, *What on earth?* He was standing in her personal space and she was not in the mood to back away...well, didn't want to. *I should be ashamed to look at him right now.* She took in his red long sleeved slim-fit shirt and black pants, and resisted the urge to sigh. *Looking his wonderful self. Hope he has forgotten about my little tirade.*

"Ladies!" he greeted them in a lazy drawl, equally caught up with Gabrielle.

"Hey, Blake!" Vivian smiled at him as she walked away. "See you guys around."

"See you around, Viv," Blake responded but his eyes were still on Gabrielle.

"Bye!" Gabrielle said looking away from Blake.

"Are you doing alright?" Blake asked Gabrielle.

The tenderness in his voice surprised her. "Yes," she said, staring at his chest instead of meeting his penetrating gaze.

"Look at me," he said softly.

She gave him a guarded look. With him standing so close, she didn't know if she would be responsible for her actions. She'd always loved to gaze into his handsome face, and now she felt even more compelled to do so with the minty smell coming from his lips beckoning to her. *Edge sideways*, she told herself, burrowing deep for self-control.

He stared down at her, with a slight smile. "Just making sure you're okay." Then as if sensing the commotion in her head, he stepped slightly away from her but force of habit caused his hand to circle her hips. When he realized what he'd done, he quickly moved his hand to her upper back. "Ready?"

Before Gabrielle could answer, a familiar female voice whispered loudly, "Get a room! But wait, I already said that!"

Across from them, they spotted Sister Sonia Solomon waving at them as she followed her husband down the aisle. Gabrielle couldn't help but smile. This was the second time that Sonia had caught them all "wrapped up" in each other.

"Behave, Woman of God!" Blake smiled at her, while Gabrielle waved at her.

"Incoming," Sonia yelled before disappearing through the door to the foyer.

They turned to see Angelica hurtling towards them.

"Uncle Blake! Aunt Gabrielle!" she squealed with delight as she group hugged them.

"Hey, my Earth Angel!" Blake patted her head while Gabrielle hugged her shoulders.

"Got to go!" Angelica told them before taking off down the aisle. "Dad and Mom are waiting in the car."

"Okay, dear!" Gabrielle smiled at her back.

Blake chuckled. "I don't know if the world is ready for her."

"Ready or not, here she comes," Gabrielle grinned as he ushered her before him down the aisle and into the foyer.

"Psalmist and Sister Montgomery!" Bishop Clandon called out before they exited the front door. "Good to see you both!" he said shaking their hands.

"You too, Bishop!" they both responded.

Bishop Clandon looked at Blake. "I missed your presence in church on Sunday. Glad you're back from your trip."

"Glad to be back. The Kansas team is really great so we were able to fix the problem sooner than I anticipated. I came here straight from the airport."

Wow! He must be tired, Gabrielle thought. Unconsciously, she hugged his waist and he lifted his hand and hugged her shoulder.

"Always glad to have you in the House of the Lord, Psalmist," Bishop Clandon said, then he smiled at Gabrielle. "You too, Sister Montgomery."

Gabrielle returned his smile. "Thanks, Bishop! Always good to be here!"

Bishop Clandon's smile widened when he saw Blake hugging Gabrielle's shoulder. He noticed that Blake

177

went into automatic mode, when Gabrielle snuggled up to his side. He wondered if Blake realized what he did, since his actions seemed seamlessly natural…unrehearsed. And if Gabrielle's reaction was anything to go by, things were clearly moving in the direction he was hoping for.

"Great Bible Study tonight, Bishop," Blake mentioned. "I like when it's this interactive."

"Yes, it was. Thanks!" Bishop Clandon agreed. "You two have a great night! God bless you!"

"You too, Bishop!" they said.

A few minutes later, they were on their way.

"Do you need a new car?" Blake asked.

"No. I've only had my car for about two years. It was making a strange sound so I took it in for servicing. It was late evening when I got there and so I told the representative to have it delivered to my office tomorrow."

"Why didn't you drive the other car?"

"The insurance expired."

Blake took his eyes off the road for a few seconds to look at her. Even though he knew she made a great salary and he mailed her a check monthly, he still needed to ask, "Do you need more money?"

"No. Noooo! That was my carelessness. I forgot to renew the insurance. I'll do so tomorrow. Vivian volunteered to drive me to church since she'd planned to attend Bible Study."

He chuckled. "Okay. At least you didn't lose your car somewhere."

"Oh, it's like that." She tilted her head to one side, playfully considering him. "Very wrong of you to bring that up."

"What are you talking about?" He remembered perfectly well, but he felt like teasing her a bit.

The first weekend when she got her new car, she went to the mall with Vivian and after they'd shopped, she

178

could not locate her car. She had to call home for him to give her the tag number. Following that incident, he bought her a miniature "Clifford" - the red plush stuffed toy dog to hang on the mirror in her car so she could easily locate it.

"You know what I mean," she pouted. "Not fair for you to bring up the past."

Laughter still danced in the depths of his eyes when he told her, "Okay. I won't."

Her heart was hammering, and the rushing sound filled her ears but his relaxed attitude boosted her confidence. "You had to fly to Kansas, huh?"

"Yes. Left on Saturday. We had a glitch in the system. Thought I would have been there longer. Thank God, it all worked out."

"Awesome! You are in charge. It would work out!"

"You trying to butter me up?"

"Noooo! You are great at what you do."

"Thanks."

Blake pulled up to the front of their home and put the car in the park position but the engine was still running. He turned towards Gabrielle and asked, "Do you need anything?"

Yes, I do! I want you to come home. She gazed at him, trying to hide her frustration. *Go ahead and tell him,* an inner voice encouraged, *you have nothing to lose.*

"Actually, I do. I need you to come home," she heard herself say.

He did not respond but continued to look at her.

She couldn't read his expression. "Blake, please," she implored.

The silence stretched between them and she gathered her purse and Bible. *Why did I put myself out there like that? Where is my pride? Getting out of here with what's left of it.* "Thanks for the ride. Have a good-."

"At times, I feel I'm partly to be blamed for what happened between you and Kanate."

Her eyes widened as she looked at him. He was staring through the windshield. "Blake, no! How could you-"

He held up his hand. "Let me finish. I left you alone many times, not only for work trips but for church assignments. Plus, our devotion times had begun to slack off. And, I also knew you were under work pressure but I did nothing to help." He had since realized he needed to have nurtured his marriage by spending more quality time with her.

"Please don't take this the wrong way but what happened between me and Larry was a mistake resulting from me not recognizing I had not dealt with the issues from my past. It's still surreal. And, I cannot believe it happened."

Blake said nothing for a moment then decided to ask, "Do you have feelings for him? Were you bored with our sex life? Did you want to try something new?"

Her eyes widened as she expressly told him, "No! No! Absolutely not! We had a great sex life. We have always had great chemistry." Her stomach tightened just thinking about the way he would kiss her senseless. "You know I enjoy and cherish making love with you, anytime and anywhere. I have no desire to make love with anyone but you...and that's still my desire." Her gaze softened as she looked at him. But, he was still staring through the windshield.

Tell me about it, Blake thought, as a shiver of heat ripped through him at the softness of her tone. He dared not look at her. It could be the end of his little charade that he was not attracted to her. He lifted his chin in defiance and his eyes stayed glued to the windshield as he disregarded the urges that were gripping him.

Sensing he had nothing to say, Gabrielle continued, "Larry was my boss, but I never saw him in that light. You know that he and I had a great working relationship and that was it."

He glanced at her, the look in his eyes sharp despite his apparent fatigue. "So, what happened?" He just had to ask.

"We were a bit exhausted preparing for our Board meeting so we stopped to drink two cans of Mountain Dew from the refrigerator in my office. We were chatting while we drank around the small table in my office and Larry mentioned I wasn't my usual self that day. And I must admit I wasn't. I was feeling a bit out of it because of what had happened between us before you left for Atlanta. However, I didn't mention that. I told him I missed Aunt Jean. He knew Aunt Jean was a mother figure in my life.

I believe he was trying to comfort me when he got the idea to massage my shoulders. At first, I was taken aback but he told me to relax and I started thinking about you and me. I was beating myself up for lying to you about wanting to start a family. Then, I thought about how I missed us not making love before you left. I was literally dying for us to make love that morning. And, as Larry continued to massage me, my thoughts began to roam in that manner." She wiped her eyes, and then covered her face with her hands. "It was over in a minute. I went into another dimension during the process. Felt like I was reliving my childhood rape."

Blake sat motionless but she could tell that he was thinking about what she'd said.

She hoped she'd adequately answered his questions because she knew they were at a critical juncture. It was important that he understood what had transpired between her and Larry, if there was ever going to be a future for their marriage.

"Do you think he has feelings for you?" Blake asked.

"I doubt it strongly that Larry has feelings for me," she answered. "As you know, he's married and from our brief conversations, I gathered that he loves his wife. I never saw him as the kind of person who would do that sort of a thing."

"Has he tried to contact you?"

"Yes. Initially to apologize and to beg me not to tell his wife."

"Did you?"

"No. After that call, I hadn't seen or heard from him in months but well over a month ago, I saw him in Talpher Supermarket and left before he could hold a conversation with me. He called from an unknown number later that week asking for a meeting. His therapist thought it was necessary."

"Do you want to meet with him?"

"No. Although, I wouldn't say never. Right now, Larry needs to go on living his life. I told him that I would report him to the police if he called again."

Their eyes met, but from the faraway look in Blake's eyes, she knew he'd turned inward.

"Okay," he murmured.

And, once again the silence stretched between them…but this time it was uncomfortable.

"How will you prevent it from happening again?" he asked, eyeing her.

"I have gone through months of therapy with Dr. William Thayer and I realized that my childhood issues were causing me to behave in a manner contrary to the plan of God for my life. I believe with Dr. Thayer's help and God's guidance, I now have a firm grip on my emotions." She paused feeling she'd put her innermost thoughts in the open. Yet, she still felt the need to say more. "2 Chronicles

16:9 states, "For the eyes of the Lord run to and fro throughout the whole earth, to show Himself strong on behalf of those whose heart is loyal to Him...," and my daily prayer is, Lord, let my heart be perfect before you so you can show yourself strong in my life. I have purposed in my heart to walk in alignment with God's will for my life. The truth is, as much as I love you, I realize that I have to love God even more for us to live a victorious married life."

He nodded his head in agreement. "Have you ever been in a similar situation?" He looked away as if just asking the question brought him pain.

"No. Apart from when I was raped. I know no other man except you."

He exhaled. "I'm sorry about what happened to you with Kanate. I'm sorry too for not extending forgiveness to you before I'd left for Atlanta. That may have stopped this debacle. If it's any consolation to you, I wanted to make love with you too that morning before I left for Atlanta," he confessed. "I just couldn't put my pride aside and forgive you."

She nodded before admitting, "I cannot see myself making love with anyone but you. I..." she paused to gather herself, "I love you," she added. Since nothing came from Blake, she continued. "I am not proud of what occurred with Larry. On my good days, I feel embarrassed and ashamed of my action, but on other days..." She closed her eyes. "I have learned to depend on my favorite scriptures and the grace of God for consolation."

And in that moment of stillness and melancholy, she weighed her next move, torn between saving herself and putting herself out on the 'open range.' She opened her eyes and found his piercing gaze trained on her. She decided to hold his gaze and felt her heart racing as she took in his strong, strikingly handsome features. It was like the moment when she first saw him through the window at church. And, she still didn't mind looking at him. He was hers, had always been hers, and she desperately wanted him back.

Feeling breathless, she heaved a sigh and made a last ditch effort before her sanity returned. "I'm sorry for not telling you about my past. I'm sorry for lying to you about starting a family, and," a sob escaped her, "I am sooo sorry about my infidelity. I cannot imagine what you have been through or are going through. But, I am begging, if you can find it in your heart to learn to trust and love me again, with the Lord's help, I believe we will have a great future together." She squeezed his hand but he did not respond in like fashion. "Have a good night. No need to walk me to the door." With that, she exited his car, walked to the front door of their home and let herself in. She waved, not knowing if he was looking before closing the door.

Blake drove away allowing the tears that were brimming to roll down his cheeks as he digested their conversation. He still felt the pangs of pain in his heart which her infidelity had created. But, he also couldn't handle her pitiful, broken demeanor...or his own obvious need for her. *I hate how we are*, he thought. *We're so wounded*. He almost gulped when an inner voice questioned, *"So, what are you going to do about it?"*

CHAPTER 19

AMAZING GOD

Happy New Year! Happy New Year!" Gabrielle twirled towards the dressing table and studied her reflection in the mirror. *I have come a long way*, she thought, knowing that from her calamity, her soul had been transformed, in a way that she had yet to fully understand.

She was in a great mood and ready for church in her knee length royal blue sheath dress and matching platform open toe high heels. She felt great, even though she had not heard from Blake. Not a peep from him.

Since their heart-to-heart conversation in his car the Wednesday before Christmas day, she'd literally been praying non-stop for their marriage. Notwithstanding, she decided to go 'get her praise on!'

Half an hour later, she observed Sunday School class while Sister Clandon taught the children, and then she volunteered to secure the Sunday school training manual and supplies in the church office. When she had done so, she made her way to the sanctuary and spotted Vivian and Sonia near the front pews. Vivian beckoned for her to join them.

"Good morning, ladies! A very Happy New Year to you," Gabrielle greeted them, brimming with renewed enthusiasm.

"Well, hello! Happy New Year!" Vivian hugged her. "Aren't you a sight for sore eyes!"

Gabrielle laughed joyfully, glancing down at her dress. "Me and this raggedy old thing."

Both ladies grinned at her.

"You look gorgeous, my dear friend." Sonia hugged her. "Happy New Year!"

"And, speaking of sight for sore eyes," Vivian chuckled softly. "Don't look now, but your husband has been staring at you."

Gabrielle stiffened, feeling slightly self-conscious. "Where's he?"

"Behind you, in his new favorite spot," Vivian said.

Gabrielle knitted her brows. "Where? Ohhh! The audio booth!" She winked at Vivian as she and Sonia chuckled. "I have it together. I promise."

"Well, thank the Lord," Vivian teased. "Anyway, we want you to be the speaker for the women's session at our Family Life Conference."

"Me?"

Sonia touched Gabrielle's hand. "The Lord has prepared you for a new level. You can do this. Pray about it and respond when you receive the official email from the Family Life Committee."

"You can do it, Gabs," Vivian chimed in. "Let the Lord lead you." She clapped her hands joyfully. "That way, I can have two things to celebrate at the conference - James' ordination and your presentation."

"You will definitely be celebrating your husband's ordination - Deacon James Moore," Gabrielle responded smiling.

"And your presentation," Vivian emphasized. "We are about to get started. See you after church."

"Alrighty. See you all later," Gabrielle responded.

Vivian grabbed Gabrielle's hand as she was about to walk away. "Remember to wave on your way to your seat," she whispered grinning. "In fact, get him a glass of water, he's still gazing at you, looking all thirsty."

"Behave!" Gabrielle pursed her lips to keep from laughing out loud. Shaking her head, she left a grinning Vivian behind. As she made her way to her regular spot, she bravely inclined her head towards the audio booth at the back of the sanctuary and gave Blake a charming smile.

A warm smile flooded Blake's face and he gave her a thumbs up holding her gaze. *She looks absolutely stunning in that dress,* he thought. *It must have been tailor-made to fit her curves.* A chuckle escaped him. *I feel like a school boy.* He had parked his car next to hers, hoping to talk with her after church.

Later in the service, Gabrielle sat and listened to Bishop Clandon preaching on the topic, "Create in me a clean heart."

"If you are a Christian, you are being renewed each day by the Holy Spirit," Bishop Clandon stated emphatically. "You will act upon new principles because as you read God's word daily, you will find the heart of God and the plan of God for your life." He wiped his face with a small towel that was resting on the podium. "I have a question for you," he said. "Are you reflecting Jesus Christ in your behavior?"

He paused allowing his question to register in the minds of the hearers.

"Our business transactions, our relationships, our private conversations, and indeed our lives should reflect the character of Jesus Christ," he continued. "No significant discrepancies should exist in our attitudes, whether we are at church, at the mall or at work. We must present ourselves as who we actually are in Christ."

A chorus of amens rang out from the crowd.

"So, do you bring light or darkness wherever you go? What do others see when they see you at work or school? Are you the light of God? Do you elevate righteousness and expose darkness? Think on these things," he told the congregation.

The keyboard player began to play softly as members of the congregation meditated on the sermon.

187

"We need to ask God to help us deal with our situations as only He can, before our situations embarrass us," Bishop Clandon said. "It's not what you do when the spotlight is on you; it's your actions that are done in the dark that will bring shame to you. One day your stealing and lying will be exposed. One day, your secret lust will be exposed. One day, your secret sin will be exposed, if you do not let the word of God dwell richly in you. You must live by the principles that the Almighty God set out in the Bible. Allow God to deal with your heart."

He paused and closed his Bible before continuing. "We have all done things, and said things that did not represent Jesus Christ. The altar is open. You don't need to confess your sins to me, only to God. Come just as you are! If you need special prayer, come!"

Several members of the congregation began making their way to the altar and Gabrielle felt the need to kneel at the altar. She walked forward and bowed over, weeping before the Lord. But this time, she didn't shed tears of sorrow but tears of joy because she felt thankful and hopeful. Thankful to be alive and in her right mind despite all she'd been through and hopeful because the future looked altogether promising because she was trusting in Jesus Christ. She felt a hand on her shoulder and from the corner of her eye she saw that Vivian had joined her in prayer.

Bishop Clandon paused from praying for those at the altar. "Psalmist Montgomery!" he called out, looking towards the audio booth. "I need you."

Blake quickly walked to the altar and Bishop Clandon handed him a microphone. "Sing, Psalmist," he told him. Blake mouthed the name of the song he was about to sing to the keyboard player and praise team, before he began to sing, "*Let Them See You*," by Colton Dixon.

His powerful, amazing tenor voice rang out blissfully in the sanctuary as he worshiped God from the depths of his heart while encouraging the congregation to lift their faith. By the end of the song, more people came to the altar, and some of the praise team members were on their knees.

Suddenly, a loud cry came from Blake's lips and he lay face down on the altar crying out to God. Bishop Clandon knelt beside him and prayed for him and when Blake came to himself, he felt the burden of Gabrielle's infidelity lifted from his heart. And, something else had filled that place in his heart - LOVE. Love flooded his soul. Pure potent love. A love so compelling that the sheer potency of it swallowed up the darkness that had imprisoned his heart.

"There is a shift. God is doing a new thing in your life," Vivian whispered in Gabrielle's ear. ""Behold, I will do a new thing; now it shall spring forth; shall ye not know it? I will even make a way in the wilderness, and rivers in the desert."" Vivian hugged her. "God is opening doors for you that no man can shut. Walk in the confidence that God is with you."

Gabrielle felt Vivian pulling away from her, only to find strong arms hugging her. Without even looking, she knew it was Blake. The warm scent of his cologne filled her nostril as he wrapped her in his arms. No words were necessary as they embraced, kneeling before the Lord at the same place where they first met and the same spot where they had pledged their love to each other - for better or for worse, for richer, for poorer, in sickness and in health.... They heard prayers going up for them, through the voices of Deacon Elect Moore and Bishop Clandon.

When church ended, Blake accompanied Gabrielle to her seat and she collected her belongings. They waved at a few members of the congregation as they made their way to her car which was parked beside his.

"Heard you were selected to be the keynote speaker for the women's session at the Family Life Conference," Blake told her.

Gabrielle smiled widely. "Am I the last to know that?"

He chuckled. "I saw Vivian in the parking lot before church and she mentioned it. You will do great."

She grinned shyly at him. "You think so?"

Blake watched her keenly, loving the way her hair cascaded over her shoulders. "I know so."

She placed her Bible and notebook on the back seat in her car and turned to face him. His wide smile met her gaze causing her to smile too, binding their feelings.

"I don't want to overwhelm you but I wanted to take you out, now," he said softly, leaning against his car. Her surprised expression told him that she was not expecting such a proposal. "Will you have lunch with me?" he asked.

Gabrielle smiled bashfully and looked down at her shoes. For a moment, he thought she wasn't going to respond. "Yes, I will," she said, still looking at her shoes, in an attempt to hide the tears that were springing forth.

Her heart hammered against her ribcage as he cupped her chin with his hand and lifted her head, forcing her to meet his gaze. She looked into the depth of his dark brown eyes and not for the first time, she felt butterflies in the pit of her stomach.

"You are too beautiful to be looking down," he said, smiling at her. The hint of judgment was no longer in his eyes.

She smiled sweetly back at him, her eyes clouded with longing. "Thank you!"

"Would you like to eat at Delput Seafood Restaurant?" he asked.

"Yes!" *Nice! One of our favorite spots. Great food. Great atmosphere.*

"Okay. Let's drive home, leave your car and we'll go in mine," he proposed.

"Great! See you in a bit," she responded, as he opened her car door then closed it after she slid behind the steering wheel.

Blake sat behind the steering wheel of his BMW and turned the ignition key in the lock; the engine roared to life. He pondered, shaking his head, *Did I just say, let's drive home?* If Gabrielle heard, no reaction came from her.

CHAPTER 20

GIVE ME YOU

Two hours later, Gabrielle wiped her mouth with a napkin and cleared her throat. "Thanks for lunch. I haven't been here in a while."

"You're welcome! I enjoyed your company." He smiled at her and that smile created two somersaults in her stomach and goose bumps attacked her arms.

She returned his smile, her heart pounding crazily. "I enjoyed your company as well. Glad we were able to get a private booth after you twisted the receptionist's arm."

Blake chuckled and a playful gleam appeared in his eyes. "And that's how you do it. It was going to be me or you twisting her arm, so she'd better be glad it was me."

"Yes. She'd better be glad it was you." She grinned at him, and then moved her plate to the side so she could rest her hands on the table.

They had kept their conversation light while they ate, pretty much catching up on the happenings in each other's lives.

She looked towards Blake and her heart began to flutter when she saw the tenderness in his gaze. A moment like this reminded her of why he would always have her heart. "What?" she asked softly. He looked puzzled so she filled him in. "You were just staring at me."

He opened his mouth to tell her he really liked being in her presence, but he just couldn't get the words out. Instead, he leaned deeper into the seat, and replied, "Really?" But, by the look on her face, he knew she was not buying his response. "Can't I just look at you?"

She pursed her lips, but her eyes were smiling. "You're answering my question with a question. I think you are guilty of something."

"Just a little," he told her quietly. He looked away from her then back at her again. "Let me get the bill squared away and we'll be on our way."

Twenty minutes later, he pulled up to the front of their home. The ride home was quiet, each immersed in thoughts.

"It's rude to stare," Blake's husky voice interrupted her thoughts. His head was resting against the headrest, his eyes holding hers.

Heat crept up her neck and flushed her cheeks. "I...Would..." She cleared her throat. "Are you coming in?"

He gazed into her eyes that were filled with love for him, and smiled affectionately at her. "I shouldn't," he said quietly. His passion for her was inflamed but he didn't want to go that route, at least, not right now. Not until he was sure that this was what he wanted. He exhaled slowly, and his smile widened because her response and corresponding actions reminded him that she knew him all too well.

She pouted and her eyes gleamed. "Why not?" And before he could respond, she swung her legs out of the car, closed the door, then walked around to his door and stood there waiting.

He slid from behind the steering wheel, closed the car door, and she held his hand and led him to the front door. She opened the door and stepped in and when he didn't follow, she gave him a gentle tug to encourage him. He stepped inside and closed the door.

Leaning against the front door, he pulled her close and hugged her from behind, his hands clasping her waist. He then buried his head in her hair and comforted himself with its scent, raining feathery kisses on the top of her head.

"Gabby." He murmured her name gently between kisses.

"Hmm."

The husky sound of his voice vibrated in her ear and in that moment heat sizzled up her spine. She dropped her purse on the ground and clasped her hands loosely around his neck, pulling him closer to her. *This is where I belong. Lord, please make him come back home*, she thought, enjoying his closeness.

He felt her flushed skin burning against him as full fever raged through his body, but he reminded himself that they shouldn't take that route. His body was ready but mentally he was not ready, not ready to let himself go again. "I missed you," he told her quietly, "but, I can't… not right now." Then, reluctantly, he released her from their embrace.

She faced him and exhaled loudly, attempting to get her breathing under control. "Okay. Well, I'll see you sometime."

With amusement twinkling in his eyes, he grinned at her. "It's like that. You're just going to throw me out."

"Oh! Oh! I thought you were leaving. Remember, I had to practically drag you in here."

"Stop. Nothing like that."

She grabbed her purse from the floor. "Want to chill out with a movie."

"Sounds good," he said, taking off his jacket and removing his tie.

"Let me make tea, while you find the movie."

"That I can do."

A few minutes later, she cuddled up at his side on the largest sofa watching "Avatar." Not long after, they both fell into a peaceful slumber. He was awoken by the ringing of a phone in the distance.

"Your phone..." Blake started, and then paused when he realized they had been sleeping in their usual positions. He was lying on his back with one arm draped around her shoulder and she was resting on his chest with one leg loosely wrapped around his waist. She stirred moving closer to him, and he scolded himself for accommodating her. *You're not ready.* He willed her back into a deep sleep so he could deal with the intense desire that was building like fever in his loins.

Yawning and rubbing her eyes, Gabrielle shifted again, pressing herself into the warmth of his lean body, a strand of her hair tickling his lips. Blake sucked in his breath as his body responded to her nearness. Simultaneously, every nerve in Gabrielle's body tingled to intolerable heights and she arched closer to him, needing to feel every inch of him. Her heart quivered wildly with frantic warnings and she sat up, throwing her legs on the ground.

"I'm sorry," she muttered, not looking at him. "I didn't mean to."

Blake avoided that conversation. "Your cell phone was ringing."

"Okay. Let me see who was calling." Gabrielle wandered off to the bedroom, glad for an escape route to hide the storm that was raging within.

When she returned to the living room, Blake was ready to go. "Thanks for a wonderful afternoon." He smiled at her, ignoring the escalating intensity of his needs...and hers.

"Thank you, too," she played along, following him to the front door.

Blake held the door handle, his back to her and in a split second he turned and covered the short distance between them and scooped her up in his arms. The eager rumblings in his heart he could no longer ignore.

The moment their bodies touched, powerful surges of longing coursed through them. A weak whimper escaped her lips as he lowered his mouth to hers, gently kissing her then steadily deepened its pressure. Wrapping her arms around his neck, she arched upward, drawn in by the fiery intensity of their kiss.

Moments later, Blake unwillingly dragged his mouth from hers, breathing heavily. He hugged her and she leaned against him as they fought for their bearings. "I desperately want to make love to you," he admitted above her head.

Goosebumps cascaded down her spine. "I want you to," she told him tenderly, still trying to catch her breath, "but, but not like this, how we are." She wanted him alright, badly. She could feel the heat radiating from his taut body beckoning to her but she needed to know where their marriage was heading. He needed to move back home…and be her husband, again.

She felt his hand caressing her hair before his fingers moved slowly down her cheek to her chin, and tilted it, perfectly aligning her lips with his. A smile tugged at his mouth as his eyes traced her face. "You are beautiful," he said huskily.

"Thanks." She smiled at him and ran a hand lovingly across his cheek, bringing his face even closer to hers.

His body stirred at her touch and a guttural groan escaped him. "Let me leave before we do something we'll regret," he said breathlessly. And before she could utter a word, his lips descended on hers again, teasing and nipping her lips and then kissing her senseless.

When he finally let her go, she fought to get a handle on her breathing. Her heart started thumping and her breath caught when he lifted her in his arms and started walking. He entered the living room and placed her on the sofa, her head falling back onto a cushion. He leaned over her. "I love you," he whispered against her moist lips.

She opened her mouth but no words came.

He smiled at her as she gaped at him, disoriented and trembling yet enjoying the afterglow of their kisses. "I will let myself out. I'll be back soon." He drew in a much needed breath, and with that he left.

Overwhelmed with emotion, Gabrielle laid there staring at the ceiling…dumbfounded. A single tear rolled down her cheek as the words, 'I love you,' joyfully resounded in her head.

CHAPTER 21

FULLY EMPOWERED

Blake glanced anxiously at his watch, noting that he had left Gabrielle about two hours ago. *She didn't respond to my text message. Hope she's alright.* His attention flickered between wanting to go back to Gabrielle and sitting in what should have been a short meeting with other members of the Worship and Arts Ministry, which Bishop Clandon was moderating in the sanctuary at church.

Suddenly, his heart rate picked up speed. And, it was in that moment that he realized how deeply he needed Gabrielle. *I love her,* he conceded to himself. He smiled inwardly - the confident smile of a man who was in love with his wife.

"Any other business?" Blake heard Bishop Clandon ask.

No hands were raised.

"Great! If all minds are clear then let us pray and get out of here."

After the prayer, there was a short line of people who wanted to speak with Bishop Clandon, including Blake.

"Psalmist Montgomery," Bishop Clandon called out, as Blake waited on the pew. "I'll see you in my office in a few minutes."

"Okay, Bishop," Blake responded before making his way to the foyer. As he entered the foyer, he saw Zoe leaving the church office. He'd seen her in the distance at church but since their incident, she'd been avoiding him.

Zoe slowly approached Blake, a nervous smile playing at the corners of her lips.

"Hey, Zoe," Blake greeted her.

"Blake," she said, staring at him.

For a moment, he thought he had grown horns. "Are you doing okay?" he ventured to ask.

"Yes. I'm okay." Her eyes registered surprise, seemingly not understanding why he was still talking to her.

He watched her as she bit her bottom lip, pondering before she spoke. Whatever she was about to say seemed to be taking a lot out of her.

"Sorry about the other day," she said finally.

"That's okay. No hard feelings."

"Please don't mention it to anyone," she begged, "I was having a moment. I'm better now."

"Okay." Blake nodded, fully well knowing that Zoe was only embarrassed about his rejection of her little performance. She was nowhere near ready to change her lifestyle.

"Have a good evening," Zoe said, as she headed out the door.

"Thanks! You too," Blake responded, taking a seat in the foyer.

Ten minutes later, Bishop Clandon entered the foyer and Blake accompanied him to his office.

"I heard the excitement in your voice when you called," Bishop Clandon smiled at him. "I take it you've received a breakthrough regarding your situation."

"I believe I have." Blake returned his smile, eyes glistening. "But, it seems my heart and head are not in alignment."

Noticing the joy in Blake's countenance, Bishop Clandon sent up a silent praise for him. *He looks like an overcomer. A champion.* The clouds of doubt and despondency had shifted and he'd been set free. "Have you forgiven Gabrielle and released the anger you felt towards her?"

"Yes! Thank God!" Blake said. "I want to go back home to continue our marriage."

"Great! Forgiving her has freed you from the emotional baggage. You are empowered for an even better relationship with her."

"What if she does it again?" Blake blurted out.

"What if she doesn't?"

Blake looked sharply at Bishop Clandon then let out a troubled sigh. "I would feel like such a fool if she does it again. I couldn't live with myself if it happened again," he disclosed, obviously tortured by the thought.

"Have you spoken to her about that?"

"Yes. And, I am satisfied. The Lord has been working in her life through the situation." He was glad that Gabrielle was upfront with him when he'd asked her a series of questions surrounding her infidelity. He'd even surprised himself that he had listened instead of arguing with her and aggravating their situation even further.

"But you would be more comfortable if she signed it in blood, wouldn't you?" Bishop Clandon asked smiling slightly.

"Something like that," Blake agreed. "My heart is way more fragile than I had realized."

"You have to trust God that it won't happen again. Your confidence is in God, not in Gabrielle. One thing is sure, you cannot keep carrying around this fear. It will slowly eat away your soul, eat away the fabric of who you are, your foundation and without a foundation you will crumble. Plus, even if you leave Gabrielle, who is to say your next relationship will be better? It will certainly not be, if you take the pain of this situation into your next relationship."

Blake nodded. "True."

Bishop Clandon watched him for a moment. "Sometimes, we wish we could foretell the future. We all want assurances in life. But, the only assurance we have is our faith in the Lord, Jesus Christ. We have to believe that whatever happens in our lives, God will take us through and we'll come out on top." He leaned back in his chair and eyeballed Blake. "Your actions tell me that you love Gabrielle. If you didn't, you would not have been so hurt about the whole situation. I know you are captivated by her persona but I believe you actually love her deeply and with her, you've experienced a love that very few will discover. If you didn't love her, you would have divorced her in a heartbeat. Now, you've found it in your heart to forgive her. The question you need to ask yourself is - Can you trust yourself to continue loving her without punishing her every day for what she did?"

Blake thought for a moment. *I do love her and being attracted to her is beyond question.* But, he wanted Bishop Clandon to just say, yes. Go ahead and continue your marriage. He wanted Bishop to take away the burden of making that decision from him…because he was afraid. Afraid to put himself in the same position to be hurt again. But, from the looks of things, that decision would continue to rest with him.

"See this scar near my wrist," Bishop Clandon called for Blake's undivided attention. "I'll always have this scar. It's a reminder to never ever put my hand near a flame again. When the time comes each year, you will remember what had occurred between you and Gabrielle. Let that be a period of thanksgiving for your marriage, knowing that the pain of the past no longer dictates the present moment and therefore no longer controls your future. You know who holds your future and you know who holds you hand."

Blake looked thoughtful. *I am ready to give the Lord full control of my future.*

Bishop Clandon seemed to have read his mind. "Ask God to reprogram your brain where Gabrielle is concerned. God has given you the grace and anointing to move through this season of your life. Every struggle you have survived strengthens your endurance. Every setback you have faced is an opportunity for new beginnings…for trusting God will produce new beginnings far beyond your own imagination, and a future well worth striving towards. You are wired to handle this, wired to be victorious in this situation." He smiled at Blake. "Sometimes, you have to decide to love again to change the end of your story. So go ahead, allow the Lord to take control of your future."

Blake returned his smile then stood up to signal his impending departure. "Thanks, Bishop! I cannot thank you enough," he said, extending his hand for a handshake.

"Thank you, Son." Bishop ignored Blake's hand and walked around his desk to give Blake a quick hug. "God bless you." He released Blake from the embrace but Blake stood rooted to the spot…all choked up.

For a moment Blake said nothing, trying to get his thoughts together to thank the man of God who had walked with him and sometimes carried him through what had been the most physically, emotionally, and mentally exhausting period in his life. Shoving his hands into his pants pockets, Blake lifted grateful eyes to Bishop Clandon. "Thanks for all you did…to bring me back to life. Words cannot express how grateful…"

Bishop Clandon patted his back. "I know. And, I understand. It was my pleasure." He smiled at Blake and attempted to lighten the moment. "It's going to be a happy New Year."

Sparks of excitement and anticipation lit Blake's face. "Yes. It will be. All the best for the New Year!"

"You too, Son! You too," Bishop Clandon managed to get out before Blake left his office.

An hour later, Blake reclined on the small sofa near the window in his bedroom. A slight smile curled his lips and his eyes glimmered as he glanced at his packed bag near the bedroom door. He had written a thank you note to Quincy and Janie and placed it on top of his bag so he would remember to place it on the kitchen table, before leaving.

His smile widened and his eyes danced with delight. He was ready for his next big move but he knew he had one last thing to do – pray. So he kneeled before the sofa and prayed.

"You are worthy, oh Lord! You are great, and mighty, and I honor You with all that I am. Lord, the scripture states, "There is no fear in love; but perfect love casts out fear, because fear involves torment. But he who fears has not been made perfect in love." I pray, Lord, that you will perfect me in Your love so that fear will not hold me in bondage. I declare that you have not given me a spirit of fear but a spirit of power, love and a sound mind. Help me, Lord, to understand that Your amazing love for me far exceeds whatsoever I face now and in the future.

Lord, I submit myself to You as I go home to my love, my wife - Gabrielle Sophia Montgomery. Enable me to love and reverence her. I admit, Lord, that I can only do this with Your help. Give me a fresh perspective, an optimistic attitude, and a rehabilitated, rejuvenated relationship with her. Help me to see her through new eyes -

eyes of love and compassion that hold constant joy, appreciation, and acceptance.

Lord, help Gabrielle to let go of her past completely. In the name of Jesus Christ, I declare that she is delivered from any hold that her past has on her. Renew her mind, Lord, through the workings of Your Holy Spirit and Your Word. Help me to understand and support her and the calling that You have placed on her life.

Father, in the name of Jesus, I declare that Your original plan and purpose for our marriage still stand. May our commitment and love for You and for each other grow stronger daily. Lord, I trust you to transform us and make us into the husband and wife You have called us to be. Breathe new life into our marriage and Father, give Gabrielle a new husband, and let it be ME. Thank you, Lord for this new season in our lives. In the name of Jesus Christ, Amen."

CHAPTER 22

UNDENIABLY YOURS

Didn't he say he would be back soon? So much for that, Gabrielle mused some six hours after Blake had confessed his love for her. She hadn't heard from him and was feeling rebuffed. *Did he change his mind?* All sorts of unwanted emotions were running through her mind as she slid under the comforter in bed.

She'd finally gotten over the knots in her stomach following his visit, showered, dressed in her nightwear, and tried to comfort herself with her favorite scripture, Psalm 91. Yet, she still felt disgruntled, even a little terrified. She was pushing aside the panic that threatened to consume her when the scripture - *"You will keep him in perfect peace, whose mind is stayed on You, because he trusts in You,"* entered her mind and her deliberations slowed somewhat.

Just then, the chiming of the doorbell broke her trend of thought. She glanced at the clock on the dresser across the room. *Who could be ringing my doorbell at 10:35 PM?*

Slipping into a robe to cover her negligee, she waddled to the front door, flipped on the patio light and looked through the peephole. She could scarcely believe her eyes. Quivers of emotions - joy, shock, annoyance, anger - ran through her head. Blake was standing on the patio, looking handsome in a pair of blue jeans and a red polo shirt, and smiling as if he knew she was staring at him.

She yanked off her night cap, stuffed it in the pocket of her robe and fluffed her hair, before jerking the door open.

He smiled proudly at her. "Happy New Year, again! I'm coming home."

It was then that Gabrielle noticed the bag at his feet. Suddenly, a gut-wrenching cry left her and she ran back into the living room.

Flabbergasted, Blake stood on the patio, trying to wrap his mind around what just happened. He certainly had not expected such a response. Pulling his bag inside, he locked the door and went in search of Gabrielle. He found her wrapped around a pillow on their king-size bed.

"Gabby," he called out softly, looking down at her from the bedside.

She stared at him with a dead look in her eyes and didn't respond.

"What's wrong?" he asked. "Didn't you get my text message?"

Anger erupted in her. "What do you want, Blake? Why did you come back? To punish me?"

Blake sat on the bed and reached out a hand to touch her shoulder.

"Don't touch me!" she rasped, thrusting out her chin. "Am I your toy?" She rolled off the bed, away from him, and stood glaring at him. And with defiance flashing in her eyes, she asked, "Did you come back to play with my emotions? To show me what I'm missing, so I would want you."

"Gabby, don't say-" He tried to calm her.

"Well, you've succeeded." She glowered at him. "I miss you and I want you. There you have it! Are you satisfied now?"

Blake shook his head in disbelief. *How did we get here?* "Gabby, stop it!"

He stood up and moved away from the bed, his back to her. "You know, I'm not like that." He spun to face her, and then had to steady himself. *Oh, that pink negligee.* She had dropped her robe on the floor and was standing before him in her pink negligee, and he couldn't take his eyes off her.

She watched as his eyes travelled down her body, scanning and digesting every inch, before testily telling him, "Isn't this what you are here for? Go ahead!"

"Don't say that," Blake said quietly.

In one minute, she had thrilled him and in the next, pierced his heart. He reasoned with her. "I sent you a text message to remind you I would come by later. Didn't you get it?" When she didn't respond, he continued, "I had a meeting at church that I couldn't get out of. Bishop Clandon is reshuffling the Worship and Arts Ministry for the New Year. After that, I had to go get some of my stuff. Tomorrow is a holiday and I just wanted to be home with you."

Nearly weak with relief, she moved to sit on the bed, her mind processing all he was saying. "I don't even know where my cell phone is," she murmured, staring blindly past him. *Did he say, spend tomorrow...with me?* A jolt of happiness welled up in her chest.

He took her robe from the floor, shook it a little to remove any dust, and draped it around her shoulders. "When I left here today, I told you that I love you and I meant it," he said passionately. "I realized I don't have all the answers to the questions about what transpired in our marriage but one thing I am certain about," he paused, taking a deep breath, "I cannot live my life without you. You are my plan A, my only plan and I intend to spend the rest of my life with you, Gabrielle Sophia Montgomery."

Her heart sprang to her throat and she lowered her gaze to the floor, grappling with the words she'd longed to hear, yet feeling undeserving. But he'd anticipated her emotional state so he dropped to his knees in front of her. "There is absolutely nothing else that you can do to show me you love me," he told her gently. "And please stop

207

looking on the floor. It's not your best look and you don't wear it well."

She pulled in a shaky breath, nibbling timidly on her lips as she watched him, the husky sound of his voice further rattling her already nervous stomach.

"I have forgiven you, Gabby. Stop punishing yourself. Let it go. Let's live and make every day count."

Her mouth opened and closed a few times before she found her voice. "Okay. Let's live and make every day count." She gave him a slight smile.

Blake stood up, returning her smile. "Group hug!"

She observed him coyly for a few seconds then pulled in by his irresistible appeal, she allowed herself to be wrapped in his arms. Her hot breath against his neck caused him to tighten his hold on her waist. For a moment, he was motionless, not wanting to rush her but when she wrapped her arms around his neck and stretched closer, he knew she was ready.

He drew back and gazed at her with the I-adore-you-look which she knew only too well. "I love you," he said.

Her body temperature soared at the flood of desire in his eyes. "I love you, more," she confessed before surrendering her heart to him.

Subduing his smoldering yearnings, he gently took her face in his hands, and ever so tenderly kissed her to allow her to set the pace.

Her body quivered and she couldn't help the urgent moan of pleasure that emanated from her lips. She wrapped her arms even tighter around his neck, urging him to deepen the kiss.

"Nooo!" she protested when he dragged his lips away from hers. She frowned impatiently at him while trying to slow the thumping of her heart.

His face flushed, he gazed down at her with a potent mixture of tenderness and desire. Passion radiated from every pore of his body, his chest rising and falling rapidly. "Sorry, I needed to look at you," he said lovingly.

She melted as his warm hands wandered up her back with agonizing slowness, sending tremors of desire gushing through her.

He smiled as he gathered her closer in his arms then kissed her like he'd been longing to since the moment he'd laid eyes on her pink negligee. She groaned loudly, reminding him that her plush, beautiful lips were made for kissing. And, he'd mastered the art of kissing them - unreservedly, deeply, fiercely, and passionately - just the way she liked it.

She didn't hold back. She showed her appreciation, hungrily accepting his kisses, and returning the favor with raw passion that he never knew she possessed. He relished every second of it, groaning wantonly from the sensations racing up and down his core. Absolutely nothing could take him away from this moment of pure bliss.

Nothing.

Submerged in a cocoon of long awaited escalating desire, they melted against one another. With the longings in their hearts drowning out the brokenness and ugliness of yesterday, they were ready to give themselves to each other again.

She shuddered as he lifted her and placed her on the bed. She couldn't wait for him to join her. And, he did. A flash of heat exploded through their tightly knitted bodies as they began to kiss each other again with wild unrestrained hunger only matched by the accelerating rhythm of their bodies.

She fought for her bearings as he broke their kiss and gave her a warm smile, his eyes blazing with an extraordinary fervor.

"I love you and I will always love you," he said softly, his thumb tracing her lips.

She blushed beautifully, taking in the vulnerability in his gaze. "I love you, too," she said softly, knowing he had allowed her to see his own sincere need for her.

With that, his head dipped towards her lips again, crushing his lips to hers, and exploring her mouth with unbridled passion. Trembling in anticipation, she kissed him back with equal intensity, for she knew Blake Paul Montgomery had finally let her into his heart again. He was ready for love and she would happily give it.

EPILOGUE

SPRING CELEBRATIONS

Spring! "It's turning out to be my favorite season," Gabrielle murmured, tilting her head to enjoy the cool breeze that was sweeping through the back patio. She stepped outside to view the evening clouds framed by clear, beautiful light blue skies against the serene landscape.

"Thank you, Lord!" she whispered excitedly. "I exalt You above all else. I praise You, honor You, and adore You! You are great and worthy to be praised!" With that, she proceeded to sway in the breeze, dancing before the Lord to music only she could hear.

"Honey, I'm home," Blake called out, dropping his work bag on the sofa in the living room. When no response came, he went in search of Gabrielle.

Lost in the moment, she did not see Blake watching her with sheer admiration. *She's at it again.* He chuckled softly. *She's definitely up to something. Um-hum! Looks serious too.* "Hello there!" he called out to her. "Getting your praise on?"

"Good evening, my love." Her sweet, breathtaking smile started in her heart and blossomed on her face as she walked towards him. "Just doing a victory dance for things to come."

There was no way he could control his response to the happy twinkle in her eyes that she sent floating through the breeze towards him. A warm smile lit his face and he scooped her up in his arms. "You know I like to celebrate. Hope you left a spot for me on the dance floor."

"I sure did. You'll be front and center stage."

And before he could respond, she cupped his face between her hands and kissed one cheek then the next, then pecked softly at his lips before kissing him thoroughly.

He drew in a shaky breath when she released his lips. "I'm beginning to love this celebration." His hands caressed her back. "So, what are we celebrating?"

"A very special occasion," she said, pulling out of his arms to close the patio door.

"Special occasion?" His eyes narrowed slightly, curiosity mixed with interest in his gaze as he waited on her.

She took him by the hand and led him towards their bedroom.

He mentally ran through the dates of their special occasions, hoping he hadn't forgotten any of them. "Aren't you going to tell me?"

"You'll find out soon enough," she responded, then giggled as his strong arms clasped her waist, picking her up from behind and letting her legs dangle. She squealed as he dropped her on the bed then stretched out beside her, his head propped up on one folded arm. "What's going on?" he inquired.

"Nothing," she grinned at him.

He tucked a lock of her hair behind her ear then intertwined their fingertips. "Something is up and I intend to find out," he said, brushing his lips across hers. And when she didn't budge, he began nibbling on her lips.

She squirmed beneath his lips, reveling in the warmth they provided. "Okay! I'll tell you," she managed to get out through uneven breaths.

"Tell me," he urged, his thumb stroking her lower lip.

Her eyes welled up with tears. "I love you."

His heart warmed towards her. "I adore you," he said in a deep, throaty whisper that hummed through every nerve in her body. "You make my heart glad."

His confession took her breath away and tears ran down the sides of her face. She'd wondered if he would ever have the courage to utter those words to her again. She reached up and gently touched his face, inwardly counting her blessings. "You make me so happy. Thank you for loving me again. I can't wait to share your love with our child."

His heart jolted. "Our child? We're pregnant?"

"Yes," she grinned at him, delight bubbling up within her. "We're pregnant."

His smile grew as joy and triumph broke out across his face. "Gabby!" Dizzy with excitement and expectation, he covered her face with light kisses. "How far along are we?"

"Six weeks," she told him, before winking at him. "I'm hoping for a girl."

He eyed her. "I bet you are."

"Victoria," she told him, "I want to call her Victoria."

A smile danced across his lips. *Girl. Boy.* He was just grateful for any new addition to the family. Since their coming together, he deliberately had not mentioned adding to the family and was content to allow her all the time she needed to prepare for motherhood. He was so glad he'd set aside his heart's desire and put her first, the only woman he'd ever loved. Now, they had two events to celebrate this spring - the news of her conception and their fifth anniversary in Paris. The first event she knew about but the second event, he would tell her about later.

Suddenly, he leaped off the bed and began to do his victory dance, hollering, "Thank you, Jesus!"

Her pulse quickened and she broke out in giggles as he danced towards her, his smile stretching from ear to ear.

"Come here!" he cooed, leaning over her.

She wrapped her arms around his neck and he lifted her off the bed, bringing her snugly to him. "I love you so much," he exclaimed, before capturing her lips with his.

213

She felt cherished and adored.

He released her lips and she opened her eyes to find him gazing at her.

"What?" she grinned at him.

"Thank you!" A satisfied smile tipped his mouth.

"Oh, Honey!" she gushed as he kneeled at her feet, lifted her blouse, and stared at her belly.

"Hello, Victoria! This is your Dad and I can't wait for you to get here," he said, gently massaging her belly with his hands, and then tenderly kissing it.

Soft moans escaped Gabrielle's lips as powerful emotions shot through her and an edge of excitement laced her belly. Instinctively, she hugged Blake's head while observing him in conversation with Victoria. One day, she would be sure to tell Victoria Paulina Jeanette Montgomery that her father and mother created victory dances, honoring her life before God.

READING GROUP GUIDE

1. What steps did Gabrielle take to restore her peace?

2. Do you think that Blake handled Gabrielle's infidelity correctly?

3. Can you identify the strategies that Gabrielle used to win back Blake's affection?

4. Gabrielle said that Vivian had been a tower of strength and the voice of reason, many times in her life. Is there someone in your life that you can say that about? *(Chapter 11 –Sisterhood)*

5. "Lord, I don't want to be like this, she thought, gripping the sink. This sad person! I want to be at peace, Lord. I want to live again." *Gabrielle Montgomery (Chapter 13 - Courage To Believe).* Can you identify with how Gabrielle felt?

6. Explain – "Don't die in a place that was only meant for you to pass through. Be brave. Ask God for the hard thing." *Vivian Moore (Chapter 13)*

7. "…When we don't deal with past issues they become giants in our lives." *Vivian Moore (Chapter 13).* Discuss this statement.

8. Can you recall a time in your life when you needed someone's forgiveness?

9. Throughout the book, various counselling techniques are used, discuss some of the tips that were given?

10. What role did Quincy play in helping to restore Blake and Gabrielle's marriage?

11. Blake wrestled with the thought that Gabrielle may be unfaithful again. Can you understand why? *(Chapter 21 - Fully Empowered)*

12. In Chapter 21, Bishop Clandon asked Blake the following question - "Can you trust yourself to continue loving her without punishing her every day for what she did?" Is this a reasonable question? Why?

13. Which character do you identify with most?

14. Why is it so important to guard our hearts? *(Proverbs 4:23)*

15. How well are you guarding your heart?

A NOTE FROM THE AUTHOR

I am delighted to share *Shades of the Heart* with you. I hope you have enjoyed reading this novel as much as I have enjoyed writing it. At this point, I can only say, look what the Lord has done. It's been an amazing journey.

Shades of the Heart is about the courage to love in the midst of broken promises, and ultimately about the healing power of forgiveness, and the journey to rediscovering identity. This story reminds us that all of our actions and choices are driven by the desires of our hearts. To ensure that our desires are in the plan of God for our lives, we need to stay connected to God through prayer, meditating on His Word and then applying His Word in our daily living.

Note that *Shades of the Heart* is Book 1 in the *Encounters of the Heart* series. Book 2 in the series, *Mirrored Hearts* will be released fall 2015. The series is based on Proverbs 4:23 (KJV) –"Keep thy heart with all diligence; for out of it are the issues of life." Although the books are in a series, they are also stand-alone novels.

Thank you for reading *Shades of the Heart*. I pray that the story of Blake and Gabrielle touched your heart in a meaningful way. May God continue to bless you on your journey.

Don't you ever forget, you are Victorious By Design.

Happy reading!
Ann Marie Bryan

CONNECT WITH THE AUTHOR

I would love to hear from you. Tell me how Shades of the Heart may have spoken to you. And, I would also like to hear your testimony about God's faithfulness.

Please connect with me at:

Email: abryan@victoriousbydesign.com
Website: www.victoriousbydesign.com
Facebook: victoriousbydes
Twitter: victoriousbydes
Pinterest: victoriousbydes

Stay victorious!
Ann Marie Bryan

OTHER TITLES
BY ANN MARIE BRYAN

Unforgettable, My Love Has Come Along (2012)
A Circle of Love Novel

Two paths, destined to cross. Friendship, faith and love are intertwined in ways neither could have imagined. Can love conquer all things?

Find out in the heartwarming and humorous pages of Unforgettable, My Love Has Come Along.

Truth Awaits You on the Other Side (2014)
(Includes Mirrored Hearts by Ann Marie Bryan)

What happens when life takes an unexpected twist…and secrets are laid bare? Find out in the page-turner, *Mirrored Hearts*, a fascinating short story about faith and love in the face of crushing secrets.

COMING FALL 2015
Mirrored Heart
A Novel
Encounters of the Heart Series - Book 2
(The story of Larry and Rozene Kanate)

VICTORIOUS BY DESIGN
Lighting the path to your next level

You are one of a kind.

You are fearfully and wonderfully made.

Embrace your uniqueness, talents and abilities.

You are designed for your purpose.

You are perfect for your purpose.

You are Victorious By Design.

Visit www.victoriousbydesign.com for more information

www.ingramcontent.com/pod-product-compliance
Lightning Source LLC
Chambersburg PA
CBHW051502170626
46811CB00002B/596